MAP OF DREAMS

Seaside Sisters Series
Book 3

KAY LYONS

Kindred Spirits Publishing

Chapter 1

Carolina Cohen raced down the street as quickly as Pearl, her pearl-white VW bug convertible, would take her. She turned the corner, spotted a parking space in front—and the massive truck heading for the same location—and floored it. Carolina held her breath and the truck jerked to a stop as she cut left and claimed the spot with a NASCAR swerve and a slam of the brakes. "Gotta be quicker than that, dude."

"He looks mad."

The roar of the diesel engine getting the gas punched was pretty good proof of her nephew Samuel's words. "The space is too small for that monster, anyway. Sammy, hurry and get your stuff. We're late."

"I know. I told you we were late when you were still in bed. Remember?"

Yeah, yeah. There was nothing quite like having her early-morning shortcomings pointed out by an almost-eleven-year-old who wasn't even her kid. "Pardon me for oversleeping after staying up most of the night to clean because of Holland hiring a contractor."

"Your room was the messiest."

Really, kid? Really? "Yeah, yeah. Just grab your backpack and let's go."

They climbed out of the vehicle and rushed toward the school, squeezing in just under the required check-in time with a whole two seconds to spare. Carolina gave herself a mental pat on the back—until she spotted a parent figure with papers in hand and immediately realized she'd left Samuel's on the kitchen counter. "Nooo. I forgot to grab the *forms*."

What now? Could she leave Samuel and go back and get them? She had to meet the contractor at the house for her sister Holland before going to work at the pier house. Could she drive back and get the papers, return to the school and get Sammy registered, go back to the house to meet the contractor, and then get to work on time?

Her nephew shrugged off his backpack while releasing a put-out sigh, pulling papers from within. "I *knew* you'd forget."

She took the required forms from him and tried to give him a quick hug, but the kid backstepped with an expression of total horror. "Hey, I'm not the plague. I just wanted to say thank you."

"We're at *school*."

"Right. I forgot you're too cool for that now. You're still the best, Sammy-son."

Samuel rolled his eyes and zipped his backpack again as they followed the signs and arrows pointing them toward the summer program her sister Ireland had signed Samuel up for before leaving for a last-minute getaway with her fiancé.

While Ireland and Dominic were living it up on some Caribbean island, it was up to Carolina and the remaining three sisters to Samuel-sit around the summer program hours. Normally Grandma and Grandpa would've done the honors, but it was also her parents' fortieth anniversary, and their father had surprised their mama with a Jeepster trip up the coast to Maine.

"When will Aunt Holland be back?"

Nice. Way to go making her feel even more like a scatterbrained idiot. "A week or two. She wasn't sure how long this job would take."

"I hope it's soon. You forgot to get cereal again. I had to eat boiled eggs. I *hate* boiled eggs."

Kick me when I'm down, kid. But Samuel had a point. Holland wouldn't have forgotten to get cereal, because she probably would've had it auto-delivered like the time-management and freakishly organized person she was. Ireland wouldn't have forgotten simply because it was her kid's favorite. "I'll get some today. Sometime. Or tomorrow. I'll make it happen, okay?"

Holland's work trip had left Carolina to pick up the majority of the load where Samuel was concerned, and while she didn't mind, she figured it was a good way to prove she wasn't the ADHD problem her family had known her to be her entire life. She could handle herself and Samuel for a couple of weeks, and maybe in doing so, her family would finally see she was perfectly capable of taking care of herself and change their attitude about her life goals.

"Ah, man."

Distracted as was her norm, she glanced at Samuel. "What's wrong?"

Samuel lowered his voice. "Nothing."

"Come on." Since he'd lowered his voice, she followed suit. "Tell me."

"It's just… I told Mom this wouldn't be fun."

"What makes you think it won't be fun? We *just* got here."

"Yeah, but the only kids I know from my school are the super-smart ones."

"So? You're super-smart, too."

"Not like them. They read. Like, for fun and not because they *have* to. And they always ace everything. I'm *doomed*."

Carolina covered her mouth and fake coughed to disguise the laugh desperately trying to erupt while eyeing a couple of the kids prompting Samuel's concern.

How was it possible that, at such young ages, the cliques were all ready forming? Samuel was smart but by sheer appearances alone, he had a point. Where he was strong in sports and all things boy and dressed the part in his typical gym shorts and a basketball shirt, the kids he referenced looked every bit the super-smart, up-and-coming professionals kids like, well, *them* tended to be. The kind that would one day give Bill Gates and that Branson guy a run for their money.

So strong were their super-smart appearances and intimidating stares because of their confidence in their brains, her less-than-stellar school record and lack of definitive career rose up to bite her. It was all too easy to picture the kids gathered ordering her about in their adulthood. *Or owning one of the fabulous homes you so desperately want to house-sit. Yeah, wouldn't that be nice.* "It'll be fine."

Even she could tell her words lacked conviction. But maybe that was a good thing for Samuel to see? Kids these days needed a reality check from all of the helicopter parents because, no, not every kid *could* grow up and do anything they wanted. Regular people weren't astronauts. Or Bill Gates.

Way to keep it positive, Caro.

Whatever. It was true, regardless. And, yeah, she felt guilty leaving Samuel behind to face them alone when she stood there intimated by them as a twenty-five-year-old adult who'd barely made it out of high school but—

Can't be helped. You know you certainly wouldn't want to be stuck doing this on summer vacation. Hello, detention!

But *now* wasn't the time to share with Samuel that there was more to life than good grades and big mortgages. She much preferred to experience life through her travels than being stuck and weighed down by things. Pearl could hold all of her belongings and could be packed up and ready to motor within an hour's notice. She *liked* that.

No, she loved it, actually.

Who wouldn't? Being able to take off at the end of the tourist season to see parts of the States she'd never otherwise see was a good thing, in her humble opinion. Travel expanded mindsets—and that was priceless.

Finally one of the red-T-shirted adults running the program called them forward and forced Carolina's racing mind back to the moment. She stepped up with the required forms in hand and confirmed the fact that Samuel's mother was away but would be back in two weeks and would check in with them then. Once Carolina signed off on the emergency contact information while Ireland—and Holland—were away, Samuel was told to go in and join the other kids gathered in the auditorium.

"Have fun. Don't forget—"

"Aunt Frankie is picking me up and dropping me off at Aunt London's."

"And if she brings the bike?"

"I have to wear the helmet."

Maybe this kid stuff wasn't so hard after all. That was the responsible, parent-like thing to say, right?

Maybe, but you can't claim it when you're only repeating something you've heard Ireland say a billion times.

Carolina watched Samuel reluctantly join the others, and after taking a moment to stomp down the guilt she felt at leaving him looking so miserable, she turned without thought and found herself nose to chest with a man. A rather large—and more than a little smelly—man. She looked up. And up. Dang, his parents grew him big. "Excuse—"

Two seconds. Two seconds was all it took for her brain to register the extreme likelihood that the man glaring down at her was the one she'd cut off in the parking lot. Mostly because he looked as though he wanted to take her head off and she'd had a vague flash of him sitting behind the wheel of that monster truck as she'd skated into the spot in front of him. "Um. Me."

His sunglasses were pushed up on his head, and if not for his anger-tight expression, she could've found him handsome. And hot. He was clean-cut, with super-short brown hair on the sides, longish on top, with bright blue eyes, a squarish jawline and… whoa.

Was that smell seriously coming from him? *Dude.*

She discreetly sniffed and realized it positively *was* him. And while she'd mastered the technique of guarding her expressions, having dealt with so many fishermen and vacationing families coming inside the pier house after a sweltering day in the Carolina sun, she now struggled to hide her disappointment that such a cute guy, well, *smelled* when the day had only just started. A quick shower, some cologne. He could've at least put on a clean shirt.

The dirty T-shirt was paired with cargo shorts and work boots that looked hot and miserable, especially considering the high today was in the low nineties. Good grief, she could only imagine how bad that shirt would reek by then.

To keep from focusing on his… aroma, Carolina glanced down and found he held the hand of a little girl with mousy brown hair and thick-framed glasses. The blue eyes were the same, though hers looked red-rimmed and puffy behind the lenses.

Allergies? The pollen was pretty high at the moment.

Or maybe it was tears because of the awful, mismatched outfit the girl wore, which consisted of a pastel floral skirt and a bright orange T-shirt ten sizes too big tied up at her waist. Not to mention inside out. "Um, I don't think you're in the right spot."

She remembered there being a defined age group for this program, and the little girl couldn't possibly be as old as Samuel. Carolina glanced over her shoulder to the red-shirted woman at the registration table. "Are you doing summer daycare, too?"

"No, ma'am. Next."

Without a word to Carolina, the man let go of the little girl's hand and gently steered her forward with his palm at her back. But not before searing Carolina with one last seething glare that left her thinking she really ought to mind her own business and... maybe apologize for stealing the parking spot. "Um...?"

The man didn't turn around or acknowledge her once they'd moved to check in, and since he was busy, Carolina shrugged and put her feet into motion. She didn't have time to spare but she'd made the effort. Well, sort of. But if he'd turned around, she *would* have apologized, so that was basically the same thing. But he hadn't, so she hadn't, and that was on him. Right?

Carolina glanced at her watch as she walked by the principal's office. She wondered if her record for most detentions in a year's time still stood at the middle school. Or had her achievement been surpassed by an up-and-coming delinquent whose attention span was as haphazard as her own?

Shaking her head at her younger self, she burst out of the air-conditioned school into the humid, late-June sun of coastal North Carolina and climbed into Pearl.

Late. She was going to be late for the meeting with the contractor. Late for work. Seemed like she was always late.

Much to her family's annoyance and upset considering they were her employers.

But what could she say? This was why she needed to land her dream job. It was so hard to punch a time clock when her brain demanded she be a go-with-the-flow kind of girl.

SILAS FLETCHER EXITED the building as the crazy woman backed out of the parking spot and shot forward like a pinball straight out of the chute. He shook his head and muttered under his breath about school zone speed limits and parents who had no regard for safety.

He'd hoped to catch her without their kids around to discuss her driving, but maybe it was just as well given his mood. He wasn't sure he could hold his temper long enough to be civil.

Silas went back to his truck but didn't get in. Instead he walked around to the rear passenger door and cleaned up the mess of Lucy's breakfast, lost to the dirt and tools and sand on the truck's floor when he'd slammed on the brakes. The one thing she had been able to keep was the milk carton—which she'd squeezed so hard trying to hold on to it that the milk had squirted out and soaked the shirt she'd picked out two weeks ago in anticipation of starting the summer school marine biology program.

His almost-nine-year-old daughter had jumped at the chance of summer school and looked forward to this special program for months, even though the school had to give her a special pass due to her not meeting the age requirement. Luce had gotten up extra early to get ready but had been so nervous at attending the program with the older kids she'd had an upset stomach, which meant stopping on the way and going through a drive-thru to replace the food she'd hurled out of anxiety after a night where she'd sleepwalked twice. Something else she tended to do when anxious.

Since they didn't have time to drive back for Lucy to change clothes, he'd given her the clean shirt he'd put on that morning, and now smelled like a soured sweaty gym sock thanks to the one and only shirt he'd found and put on to walk her inside.

Silas did what he could to clean the booster seat Lucy was lawfully required to have due to her small size and weight and made a mental note to leave the windows down so the milk smell wouldn't be so bad as he drove around the island in ninety-degree weather.

Giving up the chore because the booster seat was as soaked as her shirt, he slammed the rear door and climbed behind the wheel.

A long day had started off badly, but thankfully his house was on the way to his first appointment, and he planned to squeeze in a stop to change shirts and grab a change of clothes for Lucy. He'd meet with the client, get the signed contract and keys, text the guys their instructions to get them started, drop Lucy's clothes off at the school, drive back by to make sure the guys were on track at the new job site, and move on to his next stop.

There. He had a plan. Who said single dads couldn't get the job done?

Chapter 2

Late. The freaking contractor was late. Which meant she was going to be lat*er*.

Carolina descended the steps to the covered carport area beneath the house, pausing long enough to put her hands on her hips and tap her foot while she glared at the road.

Of all weeks... Why had Holland been called away after scheduling repairs and a remodel with the contractor? And why not cancel them since she couldn't be here?

What did she know about replacing roofs and decking and adding a crow's nest? If the guy had any questions, she certainly wouldn't be able to answer them. Nor would she since she'd probably get it wrong and say the opposite of what Holland wanted, and then her sister would go off the deep end when she finally got back from St. Lucia.

Oh, to have a job like hers.

The high-end resale company Holland worked for was Carolina's number-two dream job. Her sister actually got paid to travel the world to the clients' private islands and homes to value and list whatever outrageously expensive property they'd grown bored of and wanted to sell.

No longer using a private island? Holland would be sent to stay there and enjoy the amenities, take photos, research, and list. Same with high-end cars, jets, jewelry, furniture, and the like. To Carolina, the only job better than Holland's would be to work as a professional house sitter, where all she'd have to do is remember to water the plants and lock the door behind her on the way out to explore.

If you remember. Distracted much?

Whatever. She was getting better at making lists to keep track of things. All she had to do was remember to actually check the lists once in a while.

She could easily see herself traveling the world and being paid to care for fabulous homes while the owners were away. She'd gone through the preliminary interviews, passed the drug tests, and since she could pack at a moment's notice, she'd applied to multiple companies that handled that type of concierge service. Competition for the positions was fierce, though, and snagging one of them equated to winning the lottery. Sadly, the odds of winning were about the same as well.

Shaking her head at the ridiculousness of waiting around for a contractor who probably wouldn't show up anyway, she headed for her car when her phone dinged with Holland's ringtone. A glance at the screen left her muttering.

Well?

HE'S LATE!

Don't you dare leave. It's taken me months to move up Jake's list after the hurricane put everyone so far behind.

HE'S LAAAAAATE.

Doesn't matter. Don't you dare leave!

Fuming because Holland seemed to have some sort of sixth sense where Carolina was concerned, she stalked toward her car and tossed her purse inside the open window. The roar of an engine turned her attention to the driveway and she gasped at what she saw. "Seriously?"

It was the truck from the school. The *man* from the school. He'd followed her home!

Heart in her throat, she waited as he rolled the large truck to a stop. His windows were down and she yelled to be heard over the powerful engine. "What are you, some kind of stalker?" Her heart rate increased as panic set in. There were way too many weirdos in the world and people who took offense to the slightest thing. *Like stealing parking spaces.* She pointed to the street. "Leave. Right now. I'm sorry for cutting you off this morning, but that's no excuse for you to follow me."

"I'm—"

"*I'm* calling the cops and you'd better be gone before they get here."

He muttered something under his breath. "Put the phone away."

She pressed the phone's emergency button to call 911 so that he could see her do it.

"Are you crazy?"

She spotted a Carolina Cove police car driving down the street toward the station located a few blocks away and waved both of her arms. "Hey! Hey! *Help!*"

The man released a mutter she couldn't hear over the engine and the blood pulsating past her ears. She rushed to where Officer Bobby Binet pulled into the driveway. Thankfully she knew all of the policemen due to working at the various businesses in town. "Bobby, thank goodness."

"What's going on?"

Officer Binet quickly got out and eyed her unwanted visitor, who cut the engine and exited his truck with a slam of the door.

"He followed me home because of road rage after I took his parking spot earlier. I told him to leave but he won't."

Bobby crossed his arms over his chest and looked way too casual for her taste. Shouldn't he have his hand on his gun or something? Push her behind him and tell the man to stand down?

"Hey, Silas."

"Bobby. Good to see you again."

She stared at the two men as they greeted each other, mouth gaping. "*What*? Bobby, *do* something!"

"She's got it all wrong, brother."

"I do not have it wrong! He got mad at me at the school and then followed me home."

"Silas? That true?"

"Not by a long shot."

"It is! There's no reason for him to show up here like some crazed perv."

"Crazed perv? Lady, for the love of— I didn't follow you home."

"You're standing here, aren't you?"

The man ran his hand over his head and down to his neck, muscles flexing as he squeezed.

"Silas," Bobby said, walking closer to where the other man stood, "what's going on?"

"I just told you," Carolina said, growing even more aggravated by Bobby's lack of concern and lackadaisical manner.

Silas held up a hand as though telling them to wait and walked back to his truck.

"Watch him, Bobby. He could be getting a gun."

"Calm down. Silas isn't doing anything of the— See?"

The man turned, holding a bunch of papers clipped together, and Carolina got an uneasy, sinking feeling in her stomach.

"I didn't follow her home. I came," the man said, waving the papers, "to get to work."

This couldn't be happening. Holland was going to kill her. The man so angry with her after her stunt at the school would have to stand in line behind her sister to take a whack at this particular mole. "W-work?"

The word emerged as a strangled squeak that sounded way too guilt-ridden for her tastes. Maybe it was the heat of the day but… she actually felt a little light-headed.

Was it possible to pass out from embarrassment? What were the odds?

Seriously.

Silas shoved his sunglasses up on his head and gave her a baleful glare. "This is 114 Seashell Lane, right?"

"Yeah, but—"

"You're Holland Cohen?"

"She's Holland's baby sister," Bobby explained. "Carolina Cohen. Carolina, this is Silas Fletcher. Didn't I hear something about you working for Jake now?"

"Yeah. Her sister hired McMurphy Construction to work on her house. I'm here," the man said, giving Carolina yet another glare, "as Jake's foreman. The crew is scheduled to start today."

"Aw, now there you go. See, Carolina?" Bobby said. "Just a coincidence that y'all ran into each other this morning at the school. It's all good."

All good? This was *good*? She'd just made a total fool of herself in front of the man for the second time that day, called him a crazed perv… and Bobby thought it was good? "I didn't… I saw you pull in and I thought— You were *really* angry this morning," she said, sounding defensive to her own ears. "I mean, where's your sign?"

"What?"

Did he have to look at her like she was a complete airhead? *Did she have to* feel *like a complete airhead?* "On your truck. Shouldn't you have a sign? So people know who you are and don't think you're—"

"A crazed perv," Bobby said, chuckling as he shot Silas a broad grin.

"I-I was going to say *robbing them* but… yeah."

Silas looked at the offending truck in question and then back to her. "This is my personal vehicle. The company truck I usually drive is in the shop."

"Well, you should have a sign," she said irritably, like the stupid sign actually mattered more than her manners or lack thereof. But if he'd had a sign on the truck, she would've immediately known who he was when he pulled in. Better still, if she'd seen it at the school, she would've known not to cut him off, and this entire disaster wouldn't have happened. "I have to go. I-I'm late for work."

The abrupt announcement left both men staring at her like she'd grown two heads, but after the run-in at the school and now this, she'd be perfectly fine if a sinkhole opened up and swallowed her so she never had to see Silas Fletcher again. Instead, she'd probably be seeing him every day for the next few weeks?

Unless he quits and then you won't see him because you'll be dead, murdered by an angry Holland who just wanted her repairs done. "I… apologize." She ignored Bobby's ongoing grin and wished the man wasn't wearing a badge—or a gun— so she could…

What? Make things worse? "The signed contract is on the counter along with the keys to the house. The door off of the patio room is open. Just… call Holland if you have questions. I should… I *really* have to go."

She hurried to her car, glad she'd tossed her purse inside and didn't have to go to the house and reappear while the men watched. She was mortified enough the way it was. Maybe if she left early enough in the mornings she wouldn't have to see Silas Fletcher?

But Holland had said all of the work would take at least eight weeks, weather permitting. But how could she avoid the man for that length of time when he was working at the house?

You wouldn't have to avoid anyone if you hadn't made such a scene.

Face flaming, she climbed into Pearl, hands trembling as she started the little Bug and shot down the driveway, squeezing between the giant truck and Bobby's cruiser with both men watching her every move.

She glared at Silas in her rearview mirror and, strange as it sounded, felt like they actually made eye contact despite the fact his gaze was once more hidden by his dark sunglasses.

He'd changed shirts, she noted. Was that why he was late? She'd bet the new blue shirt really brought out the color of his eyes now.

Carolina groaned, shook her head at her thoughts, and punched the gas.

Chapter 3

Later that afternoon, Silas walked through Holland Cohen's house and made some additional notes on the work order. He'd talked to Holland on the phone earlier, and the woman had seemed very professional and matter-of-fact. She knew what she wanted and how she wanted it, and he appreciated that she spoke her mind.

In his experience, so many women said one thing, thought another, and expected something else entirely. His ex was like that in that she'd said the right things in regard to getting married and having a family, but when it came down to it, her actions proved she wanted anything but reliable.

Silas shoved the thoughts of his ex away and focused on his job. Thanks to the conversation with Holland, Silas had gotten a bit of insight as to the living arrangements in the house and discovered three of a whopping five sisters actually lived here. All were single, though the third sister who lived here was engaged and had a son named Samuel, who was the boy he'd seen Carolina dropping off at school this morning.

According to Holland, Carolina had moved in after the

last hurricane had hit the Wilmington area as a Cat 1, and the apartment she'd lived in above the pier house sustained wind and water damage. The damage had been repaired months ago, but with Holland out of town so much, Carolina had stayed on to help with her nephew.

That support system was something to be envied. He had family in Atlanta, but all worked full-time with little time left to do more than sleep.

Silas paused by a bedroom he assumed to be Holland Cohen's seeing as how it was the master suite. The large house had four bedrooms, one of which was definitely Samuel's given the toys, video games, and general boy stuff inside.

The house was decorated in soft beach colors, but the last of the bedrooms looked like a color-filled bomb had gone off. This room didn't match the orderliness of the other two adult bedrooms in that a variety of hats and necklaces hung from anything remotely resembling a hook, and colorful purses and bags were looped over the bedposts, with brightly colored clothes draped atop the chair by the window.

Given the outfit she'd worn he'd bet his hard-earned money this was Carolina's room—and according to his sheet, this bedroom contained the closet that held the attic access. He opened the closet door to confirm it and marked the paperwork accordingly.

Silas turned to exit the space when he saw a world map tacked to the wall. Black and white pushpins dotted several spots in the US near the Carolinas and the Florida panhandle, but the majority of pins were red and punched destinations across the United States, up into Canada and Alaska, across the Atlantic to Europe, and went as far south as Thailand. Future destinations, or past? For all he knew about Carolina Cohen, the pins could represent online boyfriends.

Silas left the bedroom and moved back into the hall with a glance at his watch.

It was almost time to pick up Lucy from school, and he didn't want to be late given the rough start she'd had this morning. More importantly, he definitely didn't want to find himself battling Carolina Cohen for another last-minute parking space. Who knew what the woman would do a second time around. Or what she'd accuse him of being.

Silas left his crew working and drove to get Lucy. As he exited the truck, he spotted the boy he'd seen with Carolina walking beside another woman toward an older Jeep with the top and doors removed.

He slowed his steps and gave them time to get in. One of the five Cohen sisters? From what he could see of her face behind her mirrored sunglasses, the woman and Carolina were similar enough in features for that familial connection to be true, but this woman had an edge very different from Carolina—and much darker hair compared to Carolina's sun-kissed blond.

The Jeep started up with an impressive rumble that definitely wasn't factory. The vehicle might look old on the outside, but there was some power in that engine. Whoever she was, she didn't drive like a maniac, either. She backed out of the space and rolled down the street, talking to Samuel, bits of sound carrying on the wind to where he stood.

Silas entered the school and made his way down the long hallways to where the program was located. Several students remained and most were clustered together in small groups, though staring down at their cell phones. He dreaded the day Lucy asked for one, but for her safety, he knew she'd get it.

Unlike the rest of the kids grouped together, Lucy sat

alone on the far side of the room, nose-deep in a book. His heart sank.

"Mr. Fletcher, welcome."

Lucy looked up when the teacher said his name, but as she put her book away, he saw the glance his daughter gave the kids across the room. Would it always be so hard for her to fit in due to her intelligence?

The other kids were a couple of years older than she was on average, so the division was to be expected, but what would happen when they realized she was joining their class this upcoming school year? Or did they know now and that was the reason Lucy sat alone? Was it a good idea to let her skip a few grades? She'd actually tested out of four grades, but he'd reluctantly agreed to allow her to jump only two considering it was a new school for her as well.

Lucy gathered her things and stood, and when his daughter walked by the group, only one of the kids cared enough to lift her hand in a small wave.

"Bye, Lucy."

"Bye," Lucy replied quietly, no doubt drawing on social skills taught by the therapists she'd seen over the last couple of years. Lucy walked by him and out the door.

"She did well, Mr. Fletcher. Once she calmed down."

Silas nodded at the woman and caught up with Lucy in the hall, pulling her too-heavy book bag from her bony shoulder to carry. "So? Did you have fun?"

Lucy nodded… but he still saw the tears flooding her pretty blue eyes.

Chapter 4

"I'm not going back."

Later that same evening, Carolina propped her elbows on the checkout counter inside Carolina Cove's pier house and regarded her nephew with a frown. "Don't say that. You know the deal you made with your mama. No brain camp means no baseball camp, and you've wanted to go ever since you went to that game and found out about it." Samuel looked so sad and dejected Carolina had to bite her lip to keep from smiling. "Come on, was the program really that bad?"

"Yeah."

Because of you, she thought she heard him mutter. "What was that?"

He glared up at her from one of the nearby parlor tables scattered between her station at the checkout and the walk-up food area across from her. "Come on, Sammy-son. What's up?"

"It's your fault."

"What is?"

"That everyone's mad at me."

"Wait, what? How's that?" Carolina saw a customer

hesitate due to their conversation and waved the woman over to the counter. "Keep going, Sammy. I'm listening. Hi, welcome to the pier house. Is this all for you today?"

"Yes," the woman said.

"Remember that truck you cut off when you stole the parking spot?"

Boy, did she ever. Carolina saw the customer's attention shift from browsing the gotcha area of last-minute trinkets to Samuel and then back at her. "But that was an accident."

"It's not an accident when you do something on purpose," Samuel informed her. "That's what Mom says."

Really, kid? You're doing this to me now? "I know. I'm *sorry*. I've learned my lesson. Won't happen again."

"Good. 'Cause you made a girl named Lucy cry. And throw up."

"You made a little girl *sick*?" The woman opposite the counter stared at Carolina, her expression horrified.

"No! I mean, not that I was aware of." Other customers and browsers in the shop were now staring at her or exchanging glances. "*Samuel.*"

"What? It's true. And I don't wanna go back there. Everybody hates me now."

Carolina accepted the woman's card and ran it through the machine, getting it back to her as quickly as possible so she could be on her way and not witness what was apparently meant to be the most humiliating day of her life. "Sign at the bottom, please. Sammy, no one could possibly hate you. I'll… apologize to the girl, even though it was probably her dad who scared her when he hit the brakes. I'm sure that's why she got sick." *Gonna go down that road, eh? Blame the blameless?*

Samuel sighed. "That's not why," he said, his tone a low grumble.

Carolina closed out the transaction and bit her lower lip. "How can you be sure?"

Despite having her purchase completed, the customer waited for Samuel to finish the story as did a few others. Carolina felt her face heating due to the multitude of stares.

"Because when Lucy's dad hit the brakes, she spilled her milk, so she had to wear her dad's work shirt to school because they didn't have time to go home to change before registration closed and her dad had to go to work. *Then* one of the older girls made fun and Lucy cried so hard she threw up again."

Carolina gulped, the knot in her stomach growing by leaps and bounds. "Um… *again*?"

"Yeah. Lucy told the teacher that's why she had to eat in the truck. She got sick at home because she was nervous, and her dad got her breakfast again on the way to school. Then you took his parking spot and made her spill her breakfast."

Oh, the poor little girl! *That's* why Silas Fletcher had looked like he'd just crawled out of bed and smelled like a three-day-fishing trip when he'd come into the school? Why the little girl's eyes were red-rimmed?

Why he looked as though he wanted to strangle you?

The man had managed to hold his temper even though she'd caused multiple problems with his baby girl. She could only imagine what her dad would've done in the same situation. And that… said something about Lucy's dad, didn't it?

Even when she'd called him a crazed perv and a stalker!

Lord, help me.

"When she told the teacher *why* she had to wear her dad's shirt, the girl who'd made fun then said it was *my* fault, and everyone got mad at *me* even though I wasn't the one who'd made fun and then no one talked to me after that even though I sat with them."

Kids were cruel. But when it came down to it, Sammy was right. She was the walking disaster that had set it all in motion. "It'll blow over. I'm sure of it. But I'll apologize. And I'll make it up to Lucy. I will. I promise," she said, meeting the disapproving customer's gaze as she said the words. "Maybe… maybe Lucy would like a gift from here? A shirt? Or a toy?"

"I don't think she likes toys. She's super smart. Like really, *really* smart even though she's the youngest one there."

"A T-shirt it is." The little girl's image came to mind as she'd held her daddy's hand, and now that her red-rimmed eyes were explained, Carolina felt like the lowest of the low. Kids had a hard enough time being kids these days, and if Lucy was as smart as Samuel indicated, the girl probably struggled socially— which meant Carolina had added to the girl's issues.

Shoot me now.

"Poor thing. Honey, you make *sure* that little girl gets a T-shirt," the customer said, glaring at Carolina. "*And* a toy or two whether she plays with them or not."

"Uh, yes, ma'am. Consider it done." The woman held Carolina's gaze for a long moment as though drilling home the fact she'd know whether or not Carolina followed through with the order before the woman nodded sharply and walked away. Thankfully the other customers went back to what they were doing as well.

Carolina focused on her nephew. "Was it *really* that bad?"

"Worse," he muttered. "For real. Aunt Caro, do I *have* to go back?"

"Do you want to go to baseball camp?"

His shoulders and head slumped even more.

"Yeah."

She lowered her elbows to the countertop again and buried her face into her palms with a groan. "Then I'm afraid we both have to go to school tomorrow."

And I have to come up with one heck of a nice apology. Not only for little Lucy but her scary daddy as well.

Chapter 5

Silas spotted Carolina Cohen the moment he pulled into the parking spot outside of the school the following morning. It was hard not to notice her since she wore bright pink shorts that showcased her tanned legs and a white shirt that bared her shoulders and even more attention-grabbing skin. She topped that off with a floppy hat that said *Hello Sunshine* in pink sparkling letters on the wide brim.

Frowning, he unbuckled his seat belt and cleared his mind of the chaos that awaited them before turning to look at Lucy. "Ready?"

A small shrug was his answer.

"Come on, you've got this. Show me some teeth." His daughter forced a fake smile and he chuckled at the fact she was missing a few pearly whites.

He'd dropped her off at the babysitter's house after school yesterday and then picked her up after his workday had finally ended. They'd had dinner at the diner and taken a walk on the beach, and Lucy had found a few shells. Little by little, she'd recovered from the bad day. But today had started with another upset stomach, though she hadn't thrown up. Yet. "Today's gonna be great. Right?"

No response.

"Come on. Let's get you inside." He exited the truck and walked around to open her door. Lucy had already unbuckled and had her backpack in hand, waiting for him to help her down.

"Um, hi there. You're Lucy, right?"

Silas turned to find Carolina standing a few feet away, looking as nervous as his baby girl.

"I'm Carolina," she said to Lucy. "I'm Samuel's aunt. He's in the summer program with you."

Lucy stared at Carolina but didn't respond.

Carolina glanced at him but her gaze quickly returned to Luce. Maybe because he silently warned her not to make an iffy day worse or, uglier still, turn into a repeat of yesterday.

"So, here's the thing. I heard that I caused you to have a really bad day yesterday and I feel awful about that. I was running late for Sammy's school and late for work and… I'm sorry. I shouldn't have cut in front of you—your dad—like that because if I hadn't, you wouldn't have spilled your breakfast and been upset. I'm so sorry I ruined your morning and your shirt."

Still no answer. Carolina glanced at him again, but he didn't cover Lucy's lack of response the way he normally would have. Instead, he stood silently and enjoyed watching Carolina squirm a bit.

"Anyway, I brought you a present to say I'm sorry. I hope you'll forgive me, Lucy."

Silas glanced from Carolina to Lucy and saw his daughter eyeing the bag. His baby girl did love presents. "What do you think, Luce?"

A small nod was his answer, and he helped Lucy hop

down from the lifted truck and watched as she accepted the gift, pulling out the contents.

The bright pink shirt had Carolina Cove scrolled across the front in some sparkling print.

"I guessed at your size but I think it'll fit fine. Oh, and there's a book—it's a little old for you but Sammy said... Well, he seemed to think you'd like it. And there's a stuffie. Sammy also mentioned you liked seahorses."

"I *love* them," Lucy stated emphatically, speaking for the first time. "Did you know there are over fifty seahorse species?"

A huff left Carolina, sounding like a mix of part laugh and part shock and awe. But Lucy surprised people like that. His little girl was a brainiac.

"I did not know that."

"They're also the size of an M&M when they're babies."

"Lucy wants to be a marine biologist when she grows up," he said simply. "Luce, what do you say to Ms. Cohen?"

"Thank you."

"Oh, hon, you're very welcome. And I really am sorry for causing you to have a bad day at school."

Lucy nodded, but at the mention of school, she eyed the building like it was a sea monster about to gobble her up.

"Let me have those and I'll put them in the truck for you to look at when I pick you up this afternoon," he said to his daughter.

"Can I keep the book to look at during group time?"

"You wouldn't rather talk to the other kids?"

"No."

He held back a heavy sigh. "Sure, keep it. But don't pull it out unless the teacher says it's okay," he stated needlessly. Lucy wasn't a rule breaker. He'd actually like it if she was able to loosen up a bit and rebel—then again, he'd probably rethink that statement in a few short years.

Lucy handed the shirt and stuffed animal over but tucked the book under one arm, then surprised him yet again by awkwardly stepping forward and giving Carolina an impromptu hug. "I forgive you."

"Oh! Oh, honey, you're so sweet. Thank you. You have a good day today, okay?"

"Luce, you should get inside so you're not late."

As quickly as the hug began, it ended and off Lucy went, slowly moving toward the entrance.

Carolina watched Lucy enter the building but then turned to face him again. Silas put the gift items in the truck before gently slamming the door. "Thanks for the presents."

"Wait—"

He hesitated along the length of the large truck bed.

"I said I was sorry."

"I heard."

"But… you're still angry. Your nostrils are flaring."

"It's called breathing."

"Angry breathing."

"Look—"

"Carolina," she said, tilting her head. "We met yesterday, remember, Silas?"

He narrowed his gaze on her because of her tone and the way she'd said his name. "How could I forget?"

"See? You *are* angry. I'm sorry. Okay? Really, sincerely sorry. For all of it. For cutting you off and for Lucy's bad day and… thinking you'd stalked me and followed me home. My brain can be a crazy place sometimes when I'm stressing. If you think it's bad outside, you should try being in here," she said, tapping her temple with a pink-tipped finger.

He crossed his arms over his chest and tilted his head

to one side. "Fine. Apology really, sincerely accepted. I have to get to work. Unless you have a present for me?"

She laughed softly and nodded her head. "Actually…"

"What? Seriously?"

"Yeah. After the day I caused you, it's the least I could do," she said as dug into the oversized bag hanging from her shoulder and pulled out a blue T-shirt.

"I figured wrapping it might be… too much," she said, holding it out to him. "But I heard how you gave her your shirt yesterday and that's why you—"

"Had on a dirty one?" He shrugged and accepted the gift. "Yeah."

"And Lucy's shirt was inside out because…?"

"No visible brands or logos are allowed on clothing."

Once again, she shook her head, regret marking her beautiful features.

"The new PC rules. That's right."

She rolled her baby blues and Silas found himself holding back a smile.

"I *really* caused you problems yesterday and that in no way makes up for them, but maybe you can leave it in the truck as a backup and… forgive me, too?"

He was able to laugh about it now that it was over. "The crew arrived when Bobby was there, so he had to fill them in. They got quite the kick out of the story."

"Oh, boy," she said, wincing. "Lucy's mom probably wasn't amused either, was she?"

"She's not around, so no worries there. The guys might say something if you see them, though."

"Oh, great. Another Carolina adventure story to live down."

"Another?"

"Oh, no. If you haven't heard any of them, I'm certainly not telling you. Forget I mentioned it."

He fisted the shirt in his hand and crossed his arms

over his chest. Oh, he'd find out. Fair was fair, after all. "Fine. Apology accepted. But I'm not giving up on hearing those stories. You've intrigued me now."

She regarded him with a half smile, and the last of his irritation faded. Carolina Cohen was a beautiful woman, and despite his anger with her yesterday, today was a new day.

"Okay, well, I guess I'll... see you back at the house then?"

"You're not working today?"

"Later. Is it okay that I'll be at the house?"

"Yeah, that's fine. It'll be noisy, though."

"The noise can't be worse than sitting in London's apartment feeling the floor shake every time her coffee grinders kick in down below."

"Wait," he said, his brain finally clicking and putting the pieces together. "Your sisters' names are Holland and London?" He'd talked to Holland yesterday before his walk-thru at the house, but somehow in his preoccupation with Luce and the job itself, their names had slipped by him.

"And Ireland and France—Frankie. We were all named after where we were conceived."

"So why Carolina? Why not... America?"

Her laugh surrounded him and lit up her face beneath the floppy hat.

"That's *another* long story." She turned on her heel and walked away, and he couldn't help but notice the sway of her hips. "Maybe sometime I'll tell you."

Silas watched her go, deciding that was yet another story he couldn't wait to hear.

Chapter 6

Silas entered McMurphy Construction that afternoon on his way to pick up Lucy from school and made his way past the unoccupied desks of the secretary and accounts department to the owner's office. "Jake? You in there?"

"Hey, buddy. Come on in."

Silas pushed the partially open door and saw his friend sitting behind his desk and computer. "You wanted to see me?"

"Yeah. Got you a present," Jake McMurphy said, pointing to something behind Silas. "Thought that might help you out while driving your truck."

Silas figured something was up by the snigger of laughter Jake let loose and turned to find a handwritten sign on a magnetic board that read: *I'M NOT A CRAZED PERV—McMurphy Construction.* "Funny."

Jake completely lost it and laughed until tears leaked from his eyes. "Carolina called the *cops* on you? Seriously?"

Silas ignored the sign and the laughter he heard outside the door because of Jake's booming voice and moved to sit in the chair opposite the desk. "You know her?"

"Everybody on the island knows the Cohens. Those girls have been the talk of Carolina Cove ever since the family took over the pier house years ago after her daddy retired from the military. All the local mamas want their sons to marry them."

Silas slouched down in the worn leather chair. He had a few minutes before he had to get Lucy and drop her off at Jake's house for his teenage daughter, Mak, to watch until closing time.

"I'm just glad it was Bobby that she flagged down and not one of the rookies out to prove himself. Otherwise I could've been facedown on the asphalt." His words sent Jake into another round of laughter while Silas watched and shook his head. "You can stop that anytime."

"Can't. Oh, geez. I just pictured you getting cuffed."

Silas glared.

"Okay, okay. I'll stop," Jake said, struggling to make it happen. "But you gotta admit it's funny."

"You called me in here to laugh at me almost getting arrested?"

"No. Actually… it's about Mak."

"What about her? Is she sick?"

"No. No. She's going to talk to you when you drop Lucy off today, but I wanted to give you a heads-up because she's so nervous about it."

A knot formed in his gut and he had a feeling he knew what was coming. "She's not going to babysit Lucy anymore, is she?"

"Afraid not. She made it into that music program in California, after all."

"I thought that wasn't a thing anymore."

"So did she, but it turns out her acceptance got lost in cyberspace. She just found out she got in. She leaves in a few days. We're going to celebrate on the North End Saturday. I hope you'll bring Lucy and hang out."

Silas grimaced at the news. A few days to find a reliable, trustworthy babysitter? "I'm happy for her. I know she really wanted to get in. That's great."

"I guess. Can't say I like the idea of her so far away with the state of the world today, but the program is a solid one. She'll be in good hands. I hate it for you and Lucy, though. Mak feels really bad since she told you she'd be available all summer when she thought she hadn't been accepted."

"I understand. It'll all work out."

"Ann and I will get the word out. I'm sure we'll find a good fit for Lucy for a couple of weeks."

"Thanks. Being so new to the island, we're still getting to know people. I'm not sure who to ask."

"God knows I can't lose you because of childcare. If nothing else, maybe she could go to a program off island?"

"Maybe." But he hated that idea. Jake didn't want his teenage daughter going to California, but the fact of the matter was, he didn't want Lucy going off island. Summer traffic meant more accidents than the norm as tourists rushed to and from their summer vacation spot, and with one road on and off the island, he didn't want to be stuck in traffic while Lucy waited and fought off a panic attack when he wasn't there on time.

Maybe he babied her, but given all the kid had been through with her mom leaving and then losing everything after the hurricane, he felt some allowances had to be made until Lucy got her feet under her again and felt more secure.

"You know, another solution would be for you to find a wife."

Silas met the man's gaze, yanked from his thoughts by the words. "What?"

"Come on, man. Don't let one bad woman taint your view of all of them. Take Carolina, for instance—"

"You're insane—*she's* insane."

"Nah, she's a good girl. A little high-strung is all. And why not her? Crazed perv comment aside, she's nice, beautiful, comes from a good family. You could do worse."

She was those things. But first impressions being what they were, she was also impulsive, unfiltered, and a whirlwind of chaos. "How about you stick to construction?"

"Silas, you haven't dated anyone since I've known you."

"I've gone on a couple of dates."

"With women who sat there and sexted other men."

"I shouldn't have told you that."

"But you did. And I'm talking about serious dating. Not that online hookup stuff people are doing."

"Being a single parent—"

"Isn't easy. But look at this thing with Lucy. If you had a mate, there would be two of you to share the load and figure this out. What are you waiting for?"

"Did you suddenly become a matchmaker or something? I'm fine."

"Maybe, but if it's this hard now, when Lucy is young, think of how hard it's going to be when she's a teenager. Girls need a woman's touch. Trust me on that. Daddy's girls tend to rule daddies whereas a woman sees through the tears and drama and brings some reasoning to the mix."

"Did you just admit Ann is smarter than you?"

Jake immediately looked aggrieved. "Now don't go spreading rumors like that. There's not a doubt in my mind that she is, but I'll deny it to my grave."

Silas stood. "I have to pick up Luce."

"We're meant to be married, buddy. Like the good book says, it helps to have a mate by your side when you need a hand up. Hey, you forgot your sign! You might need it if you run into Carolina!"

Chapter 7

Several days later, Carolina awoke to thuds and hammering on the roof. Crud. The crew had arrived to work. And on one of her rare days off, no less.

She rolled over and out of bed, dragging her sleepy self into the bathroom. After a quick shower, she'd dressed and was downstairs chugging coffee when someone knocked on the door. She didn't bother calling out, but before she got to the door to answer, a key unlocked the lock and she came face-to-face with Silas Fletcher. "Breaking and entering now?"

Silas looked surprised to find her there but held up the key. "I have permission. Your car isn't downstairs. I thought everyone was gone."

Carolina realized Silas wasn't alone. "Hi, Lucy. Why aren't you in school?"

Silas shot her a questioning stare. "It's closed today due to a power outage on those blocks. Shouldn't you know that?"

"Uh-oh. Did I lose Sammy again?" she asked, making a face as she moved over to the cabinet where she'd left her phone overnight to charge, praying all the way that she hadn't slept through a call from Samuel, the school, or her sisters about the change in schedule.

She ran her finger over the screen and punched in her code to unlock the phone, sagging against the counter in relief she hoped she disguised by acting casual. "London dropped Sammy off at the garage this morning after finding out about the closure, so he's helping Frankie change the oil in Pearl. Shew. He's not lost."

He stared at her with a frown of blatant disapproval.

"Oh, come on, really? I didn't mean *lost* lost. Just… momentarily misplaced." She grinned, made a funny face, and even considered doing a jig, something, to make the uptight Silas lose some of the tension marring his gorgeousness. The man was hot but uptight and she'd love to see him cut loose.

One of Silas's thick eyebrows rose, and he stood there all tall, tanned, and broody, giving her that look of his.

"Okay, fine. Samuel spent the night at London's. My sister volunteered to take him on my days off so I could sleep in. I should be sleeping right now, except I couldn't because of the hammering. Oh, look at you, Lucy! Your shirt looks awesome."

Silas blinked at Carolina and the abrupt change in subject, and she realized she'd done it again. Recognized the expression Silas wore, because it meant in her ADHD moment, she'd gotten distracted and forgotten to do that transition thing that regular people tended to do in conversations *before* they changed subjects. Oops.

"Hammering comes with replacing the roof and adding on decks. Better get used to it because it'll be a good while before we're finished. If you want to sleep in on your day off, maybe you should stay with Samuel at your other sister's."

She planted her hands on her hips and tilted her head

to one side as she regarded him. "Mm. I guess so. Did I miss the memo about Take Your Kid to Work Day?"

Silas's expression changed from mild irritation to unease. "My sitter wasn't available. She thought Lucy would be in school, so she went to Charlotte to do some shopping for a trip."

"She quit," Lucy said without looking up from her book.

Note to self: never think a kid isn't listening.

"She's unavailable for a couple of weeks is all. I'd hoped Lucy could sit in here and read while I check in on the guys, but she'll be fine in the truck."

"In this heat?" Seriously? Even she knew kids and dogs didn't belong in hot cars.

"I'll run the AC for her."

"That doesn't work for me. Bad for the environment," she explained when his gaze narrowed. "But you're in luck because I've met my quota for losing kids today, so she's safe to hang out in here. What are the odds I'll misplace another one?"

The look Silas Fletcher shot her resulted in uncontrollable laughter bubbling out of her chest, but she refused to take his too-serious expression to heart and chose instead to focus on the little girl. "What do you say, sweetie? Wanna stay with me while your dad is working?"

Her daddy's blue eyes blinked at Carolina from behind blue-framed glasses, and combined with the humidity-teased curls around the girl's face, the picture that formed was too cute for words. She looked like an adorable Einstein-like prodigy.

"Okay."

"I don't know," Silas said. "She would be fine in the truck."

"Maybe. Then again," she said, lowering her voice, "when I was her age, my dad made the mistake of leaving me in his truck and I decided to take it to the gas station for candy."

Silas's eyes went wide. "You stole a truck?"

"I *really* had a craving for some Chewy Sweetarts."

Silas swallowed audibly and she bit back a grin.

"She'll read and be good. Right, Luce?"

"Yes."

"I'll be twenty minutes, a half hour at most, and right outside if you… she needs me."

"Perfect. We'll be here." Carolina waited until Silas murmured goodbye to his daughter and made it to the door before adding, "Hey, Lucy. You got any matches?"

Chapter 8

Silas rounded the house an hour or so later, hurrying up the stairs to check on his daughter. Halfway up, he heard giggles and paused. Was that… Lucy?

It was. His shy, quiet, much too reserved, super-intelligent daughter was *giggling*.

The sound punched him in the gut like a prizefighter. He continued on, quietly this time, hoping to catch a glimpse of whatever it was Carolina was doing to bring that precious sound out of a little girl who spent way too much time worrying and stressing.

On the other side of the glass door, he spotted Carolina and Lucy sitting on the floor surrounded by a sea of red, white, and blue. Both wore blinking flower crowns in addition to headbands with stars wobbling on wires atop their heads, oversized star sunglasses, and light-up leis piled around their necks. Carolina blew a noisemaker while wielding a wand with dangling streamers.

The boxes he'd seen stacked neatly earlier were all open, the contents scattered throughout the room like a patriotic tornado had blown through. Tri-colored banners were draped along the back of the sofa, LED lights were plugged into the walls and flashed in random sequences, and giant sequined Uncle Sam hats glittered atop the island bar and barstools.

And there in the middle of it all sat Lucy. Lucy, who hated messes and insisted on keeping everything neat and orderly to a fault, but seemingly wasn't anxious about the chaos around her because she was so involved in playing with it.

His daughter giggled again, and he shifted his attention back to Carolina, catching her in the act of making goofy faces that left him smiling as well. She was a unique one, no doubt about it. He knocked softly and opened the door. "What's going on in here?"

"We're product testing."

"So I see. You look ready for a July Fourth parade."

"Otherwise known as fireworks at the pier," Carolina said. "Lucy's helped me get things organized. My sisters will be so impressed because I'm not doing this at the last minute."

"Can we go see the fireworks?"

"Uh, sure. If you want."

"Lucy told me she didn't like the noise or crowds, but I told her the beautiful colors made up for it—and head-phones help block the big booms."

Headphones? Why hadn't he thought of that? "We'll try that." Trying it was about all they could do, because when it came time for the show to start, Lucy would prob-ably take one look at all the people and have a meltdown like she had every year they'd attempted to go in her short life. "Luce, take all of that off. We have to get going."

"But I don't want to leave."

"Hey, you got to stay longer than planned. I'm sorry about that," he said to Carolina.

"Not a problem. We've had fun."

"Luce? Get moving. I have to go check on the other

jobsites. Take that off and say thank you to Carolina for watching you."

Big tears welled up in Lucy's eyes and Silas felt like a monster. Not because she cried but because it was so seldom that Lucy actually seemed to have fun and play like a "normal" kid should. But what else could he do?

"Um, you know," Carolina said, standing, "I really don't have a lot going on today. Just laundry and decorating the golf cart and getting it prepped for tomorrow night to sell this stuff. I'll be here all day."

Silas narrowed his gaze on her. Surely she wasn't suggesting… "That's nice."

Carolina glanced at Lucy before bending to grab a bunch of plastic necklaces from the coffee table.

"Lucy, would you mind putting these back in the bag and putting the bag by the flower ones?"

"Okay."

Once Lucy had walked away, Carolina met his gaze.

"Let her stay."

"What? No."

"Why not? She's having fun and I'll be here all day."

He tracked Lucy's movements across the room. "You want to babysit on your day off?"

"I wouldn't offer if I had plans, but I really don't so… consider the offer part of my apology to go with the T-shirt," she added, smiling up at him.

It was a nice offer, and he was tempted given the work he had to get done, but she was a stranger. "I appreciate the gesture but I really can't accept."

"Why not? Wouldn't staying here be better than her sitting in your truck all day?"

"Yeah, but—" Silas ran a hand over his face and wished he had an alternative plan but he didn't. What was he going to do when Mak left for California? He'd made a few inquiries but so far hadn't found a temporary replacement. "You thought I was a crazed perv a couple of days ago."

"That's before I realized you work for Jake. He wouldn't have hired you if you're weren't an okay guy, though a little uptight. What's the worst that could happen? Do you really think I'd lose her?"

Uptight?

"Really? You think I'd *lose her*?"

The indignation in Carolina's tone forced a grumbling laugh out of his chest. "No. That's not— It's a good idea and I appreciate it, but I'll be all over the county today. And I might be late getting back tonight, depending on how things go. Not to mention the holiday traffic coming this way. If I get stuck… It would be best if she came with me."

"Everything you just said makes it clear she *needs* to stay with me. You're seriously going to drag an eight-year-old all over town in this heat and leave her sitting in your truck all day?" Carolina shook her head. "That's cruel. Call Jake or one of my bosses and get references if you like."

"Don't you work for your father and… sister?"

Her gaze narrowed. "What does that have to do with anything?"

He crossed his arms over his chest, unwilling to admit he'd checked her out on social media after their run-in. "Most family members would give their kid or sibling a good reference if asked."

"Really? Do you have any idea how hard it is to work for family? Talk about having to stay on your toes. And technically I actually work for *two* of my sisters now," she argued. "Which is actually a good point. Ireland left Sammy in my care, so that proves she trusts me, so I get double points for getting boss and sister love."

Boss and sister love? "You didn't know where the kid was this morning."

"I *knew* he was with my sister because he'd spent the night there. I just didn't know what she'd done with him after the power outage because I was *sleeping*. There's a difference."

He looked from Carolina to Lucy and back again. His too-smart daughter was blatantly eavesdropping. "Luce? What do you think? Would you rather go with me or stay here?"

"Stay here."

"See?" Carolina said, sounding way too smug.

"You won't get scared? You only just met Miss Cohen." He shot Carolina a pointed look.

"What, now *I'm* the crazed perv?" Carolina murmured under her breath.

"I won't get scared, Daddy. If I do, I'll call you."

He glanced at his watch. He *had* to go. "Fine. You can stay. But I want hourly check-ins from you," he said, pulling his phone from his pocket to get Carolina's info.

"Of course."

"And she has to eat. No skipping and saying you're not hungry, Luce. She's picky, though."

"I like the diner," Lucy told Carolina.

"Me, too!" Carolina planted her hands on her hips and grinned like she'd won some sort of victory. "See? Problem solved."

Except the diner was by the pier and to get there—"Exercise," he blurted. "She, uh, can't sit and read all day. You guys can walk. The diner isn't that far." He didn't want to think about his baby girl strapped in the back of Carolina's rocket mobile, and he thanked God that it was in the shop for an oil change.

Carolina gave him a baleful stare like she knew *why* he'd mentioned walking, and to distract her, he handed her his phone and took out his wallet at the same time. "Put in your number. Lunch is on me."

Carolina entered her information as requested and sent herself a text to establish contact before lifting her head and spotting the cash. "Dessert, too," she said with a come-hither curl of her fingers. "We want ice cream since we'll be doing all that *walking*. Right, Lucy?"

"Right!"

He forked over an extra ten. "Fine. But if you miss a single check-in, you have to refund me for dessert."

"Deal."

"Every hour on the hour," he stressed to Carolina.

"Okay."

"Lucy, you'll remind Miss Cohen if she forgets?"

"Yes, Daddy."

"Geez, chill, will you?" Carolina said, walking him to the door. "Try to remember Ireland's been gone almost a week and her kid is still around here somewhere."

Chapter 9

Silas didn't get simple check-in texts from Carolina. Throughout the long, hot, problematic day that had begun with the power outage at the school and lack of babysitter all the way up until his last stop, he received pictures of Lucy's day. The first image was of her eating avocado while sitting at the island bar in Holland Cohen's home, still dressed in her Fourth of July finery and sunglasses.

Silas stared at the image for a long moment. He didn't know Lucy *liked* avocado and there she was eating it? How had Carolina managed that? Luce was notorious for her pickiness, which didn't help her when it came to gaining weight on her too-thin frame.

The next check-in was of a twenty-second video of Lucy putting on an impromptu class on seahorses with the video flashing to Carolina mouthing the word *wow* before turning it back to his baby girl.

Wow was right. He wondered what he'd ever done to deserve such an insanely smart, fabulous kid, but he was glad Carolina had gotten through the shy, withdrawn shell Lucy sometimes hid behind to the smart, funny little girl beneath.

Hour three was a selfie of the two of them sitting in the diner with Lucy holding up a double bowl of ice cream topped with whipped cream and sprinkles. He sat in his truck looking over a supply order that had been screwed up when the familiar text tone came through, and was thankful Carolina had offered to watch Lucy so his daughter wasn't subjected to a boring day of listening to him muttering about problems.

One by one, the photos and videos kept coming. Lucy holding up a seashell, her nose covered in zinc and what had to be one of Carolina's floppy hats, the pier pilings and surf behind her, and a second one of Lucy on the pier tossing a bit of something to Pelican Pete.

Lucy organizing the Fourth of July chaos in the living room into neat little piles.

Lucy washing a golf cart.

A video of what looked to be an epic neighborhood kid water-gun fight that included Carolina's nephew, Samuel, teaming up with Lucy to battle the others.

Carolina and Lucy with soaked hair grinning at the camera, dog noses and ears filtered on.

By the time evening rolled around and his day was over, multiple images filled Silas's phone, and he'd taken the time to save them because they'd made a trying day better. Like predicted, he battled the July third traffic out of Wilmington all the way to the island and finally pulled into the drive to find his crew gone for the day and Carolina and Lucy in the shade of the carport beneath the house. Lucy held a string of blinking lights like those he'd seen upstairs that morning and waited for Carolina to zip-tie them to the golf cart.

"Hi, Daddy."

He kissed the top of Lucy's still-damp hair and hugged her. "Hey, baby. I got your pictures. Looked like you've had a fun day."

"I loved staying here."

Carolina was lying on a water float atop the concrete slowly working the lights along the base of the cart. "Aww. Well, I loved having you here, sweetie. It was nice having a girl around for a change. But don't tell Samuel I said that."

"I won't."

Silas saw Carolina struggling to hold the tubing in place while tying it and squatted down to lend a hand. "Here. I got it."

"Thanks."

"All of this is for tomorrow?"

"Carolina sells it for her trips."

"Oh?"

"Yeah. I get a permit every year, fix up the cart, and hit the streets. This stuff sells like hotcakes, and I put it all away in my travel fund. The big goal is Australia, but until I have enough, I'm thinking of driving up the California coast and stopping in all of those little towns I've read about but never seen. Or maybe driving down to the Keys. Or Maine?"

They finished that line of tubing and Lucy quickly stepped closer with the next roll.

"It goes on the other side," Lucy told him.

He straightened and then automatically accepted the hand Carolina stretched up for him. With a light tug, he pulled her to her feet but quickly caught her arms when she wobbled.

"Whoa. Major head rush," Carolina said, closing her eyes briefly with a laugh. "Thanks for the save."

"No problem." She opened her eyes and he found himself just standing there, staring into depths as blue as the Atlantic not far from them.

"You can, um… I'm good now."

Only then did he realize he still held her arms, and he released her. "Just making sure you were stable."

His stomach growled loudly.

"Daddy's always hungry when he gets home from work."

He placed a hand over his belly and shot Lucy a teasing glare. "And you always make fun. You ready to go feed me?"

"But we have to stay and finish decorating the golf cart. You're good at building stuff, and Carolina's daddy isn't here to help her with those."

He looked to where Lucy pointed at what appeared to be some kind of plastic merchandise displays before meeting Carolina's gaze. "Those go on the cart?"

"Yup."

He didn't want to overstay their welcome if she didn't want them there after watching Lucy all day, but the bins looked heavy. "I can lend a hand before we leave if you like."

"I certainly won't turn down help," Carolina said. "Usually my dad holds the bins while I fasten them on. Actually," she said, her tone changing, "I have some burgers in the fridge ready to grill with all of the fixings, *and* sweet potato fries. There's plenty. How about I feed the growling stomach in exchange for your building expertise?"

As though right on cue, his stomach growled again. Louder and longer than the time before.

"Can I take that as a yes? There's plenty since Holland and Ireland are both gone."

Lucy waited expectantly and Carolina looked so fetching in the cutoff shorts and tank top she now wore that he found he couldn't say no. What was it about a fresh-faced, wind-tossed beach girl? "Go fire up the grill while I take a look at the bins."

"Awesome. I really dreaded tackling those things alone."

Carolina high-fived Lucy and they did a happy dance

the two had apparently choreographed at some point during their day together.

"Happy to help." Carolina met his gaze and he realized in that moment how wrong first impressions could be.

"Um, Lucy, will you show your dad the pictures of what the cart is supposed to like when it's done?"

"Yes."

"Thank you, sweetie."

Carolina Cohen turned to go.

"Daddy?"

Lucy's voice jerked his attention from Carolina and he ran a hand over his mouth. "Yeah, baby?"

"Will you pay Carolina to watch me when Mak goes to California?"

Carolina had started up the stairs but paused when she heard the question. Silas focused on his daughter. "Luce, today was an exception. Carolina has a job."

"I do. A couple of them," Carolina said with a nod. "But I'm also open to the idea if we could work out a schedule. My travel fund is a *hungry* hippo," she said, winking at Lucy. "We'll discuss terms over dinner."

Discuss terms? He hadn't agreed to anything, and yet looking down at Lucy, he realized his daughter practically beamed with happiness at the thought. "I'm not so sure Carolina babysitting you is a good idea," he said once Carolina was out of hearing range.

Lucy used one small finger and pushed her glasses up her nose. "We'll discuss terms over dinner, Daddy."

Chapter 10

Thirty minutes later, Carolina stood in the kitchen while the microwave counted down and stared at the computer screen several feet away on the desk, currently scrolling through the photos of her potential vacation destinations. She'd found the photos online and added them to a file that acted as research, inspiration, and motivation to work as crazy hard as she did during the summer season so she was free to go where she chose during the off-season.

She longed to travel far and wide, but finances were an issue like they were for most people. She'd traveled within a five-hundred-mile radius of Wilmington over the winter months, and last year she'd lucked into a house/pet-sitting job in the Florida panhandle that had led her to check into house-sitting in other places… like Europe. If she managed to win the house-sitting job lottery overseas and get hired by one of the elite companies specializing in such things, well, that would be the start of her dream life. Nothing would hold her back then because she wouldn't have lodging expenses and her hard-earned cash would stretch a lot further. Maybe she should apply to less desirable locations first? To get her foot in the door and build from there?

The microwave dinged and she removed the lightly softened butter and added cinnamon to it. Like ketchup was to french fries, sweet potatoes needed that little extra *oomph* of flavor, and cinnamon butter was what kicked it over the top.

"Those smell amazing," Silas said from where he stood just inside the door. "I knocked but you were in deep thought. I let us in so Lucy could wash up. I hope you don't mind."

"Oh, no. Not at all. Sorry. You caught me daydreaming." She glanced at Silas and noted once again how adorably handsome he was in his logoed work shirt and khaki shorts. He wore his hard work the way he did his clothes, and she could tell he was the hands-on type by the muscle he carried.

The bright color of his shirt brought out his tan and blue eyes and stretched across his broad chest. One she couldn't help but think would make a nice pillow on occasion. A woman would have to be blind not to notice how attractive he was. And this time he smelled good. Despite a day's work, the air held just the slightest hint of his cologne, and she breathed it in like she had downstairs when he'd helped her with the cart lights.

"Dreaming of how much money you're going to make tomorrow selling all that stuff?" he asked, lifting his hand and waving it toward the now-organized items ready to go into the bins.

"Actually, I'm still thinking about Lucy's babysitting idea. Is that a possibility?"

Silas stared at her like she'd grown two heads. "I… have to find a replacement for Mak, but—"

"I'll take it. The job, I mean. I've been thinking I'd like

to pick up another job and today was fun. It's perfect timing, am I right? Like it was meant to be."

Yeah, Silas so didn't look convinced. Was he stuck on her not knowing school had been canceled this morning? So not her fault!

"How do you plan to schedule babysitting around the jobs you already have?"

"Well, it'll be a juggle but I think it's totally doable."

"Carolina, no offense, but this is my daughter. I'd need more than a *you think*."

"I know. That's the thing. See, there will always be someone at school to pick Sammy up whether it's me or one of my sisters. Right now you're having to drive back to school every day to get her because your babysitter— What's her name?"

"Mak."

"Right. Because Mak's too young to drive. Lucy filled me in," she said when Silas frowned as though wondering how she knew the details. "So, if you gave your permission, Lucy could carpool with Sammy since picking up one kid versus two is no big deal, and said picker-upper could keep, if it was me, or drop, if it was one of my sisters or mom, Lucy off to me for the hour and a half or so that's left until you get home from work. See? Easy-peasy."

"Drop her off… at your job?"

Carolina waved a hand at his disproval. "If I'm working, yes. Otherwise, we could come here or go do something. Anyway, even if it means her hanging out at work with me, it's not like I'm on a construction site like you are. There's a backroom behind the desk at the inn, where Lucy could read or watch television, play games, whatever. And London's coffee shop has an area for kids as well. We're very kid friendly because of Ireland needing a place for Sammy, and besides, we're not talking about an all-day thing but only an hour or so."

"Don't you also work at the pier house? I don't want her there unsupervised. Anything could happen with that many people coming and going."

"I *totally* understand that," she said, flashing him a quick nod as she stirred the buttery concoction. "So…" she said, pausing but thinking fast, "I'll talk to Ireland and work the schedule so that I'm at the inn more, where Lucy can hang out in the back room. The hours and pay are the same, and I've always shuffled back and forth between the two anyway. It works. Right?"

"I… suppose it might work since it's temporary. But why do you want to take this on when you're already working three different places?"

"Money," she stated bluntly. "Hey, you asked, I'm answering. Look, Lucy's a great kid. And if I wasn't watching her, I'd be picking up a different job somewhere else, which means I'd be juggling regardless."

Silas leaned a shoulder against the wall where he stood and stared at her with laser intensity.

"Instead of all of these jobs, why not get a single job that pays as well as the others combined?"

The timer went off and she grabbed the mitt to pull the fries from the oven. "Ha! Good idea in theory, but those types of jobs bore me to tears, and two weeks of vacation a year does *not* work for me."

"I see."

Yeah, he didn't understand. Most people didn't. "Do you like traveling?"

"Haven't done a lot of it but yeah. Sure."

"Clean!" Lucy called, walking back into the room, hands held up in front of her like she prepped for surgery. "Your turn, Daddy. Did you say yes?"

Carolina glanced at Lucy and realized the girl had heard their conversation.

"Not yet."

"Will you say yes?"

Silas gave his daughter a patient look and lifted one thick eyebrow high.

"I'm considering it."

"Mak leaves soon, Daddy. I'm too young to be left home alone."

Silas and Carolina both struggled to hold in a laugh, and Carolina turned away briefly to hide her smile.

"I'm very aware of that, Luce. Let me ponder it for a while, okay?"

Silas met Carolina's gaze once she faced them again. "You understand."

"Of course."

Silas didn't say anything more, and after a moment, Carolina went back to getting dinner on the table. "So, how about we feed your hungry father?"

"Sounds good to me. I'll go wash my hands," Silas said, moving by Lucy toward the downstairs bathroom.

"Lucy, will you help me set the table?"

"But I just washed my hands."

Throughout the day, Carolina had picked up on a few of the little girl's idiosyncrasies, cleanliness being one of them. Wasn't part of being a kid getting dirty? "Yeah, I know, but the plates are clean, so your hands will stay clean."

Lucy's expression revealed her doubts about the matter, but after a pause, she moved forward and accepted the stack of plates.

"Four?"

"One is for Samuel. He'll be here any minute."

As though conjured by her words, Samuel could be heard pounding up the wooden stairs leading to the main level, and he burst into the house.

"Is it ready? I'm hungry and the guys are waiting for me to come back and swim."

"You have to wash your hands first," Carolina stated.

"I was in Toby's pool. It's a big bathtub."

"Is not," Lucy and Carolina said in unison.

"Statistics state you should shower after swimming in any body of water due to bacteria and fungi on your skin," Lucy quickly informed them.

Samuel split his attention between the two of them before shaking his head and moving toward the half bath in the hall the same time Silas reappeared.

"Girls," Samuel muttered as he trudged by.

Silas met Carolina's gaze and chuckled.

Lucy pushed her glasses up her nose with her bent wrist so she wouldn't use her clean fingers and released such a long-suffering sigh that it made Carolina turn away or else risk being seen as she smiled yet again. Little Lucy was a miniature comedian without meaning to be.

"Luce, hand me two of those and I'll do this side."

Carolina glanced over her shoulder and spotted Silas helping his daughter set the table, and the image was so sweet she—

What? Want to pretend it's real? Yours? You don't do home and hearth, remember? You don't want to have to consult with anyone about where you go, when you go, or if you go.

She had to stop romanticizing a nice evening with a man and remember this was just the result of an apology meant to make amends that might turn into a job. *Stay focused for once, Caro.*

"I took a quick look around before I came upstairs," Silas said. "The guys have made good progress. The roof is finished, and after the holiday, they'll begin repairing the existing deck. Once that's done, they'll start on the upper deck going to the crow's nest."

She welcomed the subject with open arms. "I can't wait to get up there and see the view."

"I'm surprised the previous owners didn't have it built

when the house went up. The best view a person can have is of home."

Silence followed his words and she realized she was just standing there, staring at him, silently disagreeing. In her opinion, the best view came with new adventures. New places. *New* views. *Oh, yeah. ADHD all the way. Gotta keep the brain entertained.* "Um… if you say so. Ready to eat?"

Eating with two kids at the table was even more mind-boggling than eating with Sammy. Sharp-witted little Lucy could hold her own when it came to verbally sparring with her nephew, and Carolina laughed throughout the meal as they debated the merits of going to school in the summer versus enjoying summer break, and how swimming in the ocean was better than in a pool.

Thankfully Lucy knew the facts, and even though Carolina knew she probably shouldn't take sides against her nephew, it was good to see Sammy getting what-for after him calling her crazy when Silas asked what it was like to live with her.

After dinner the kids asked to play a video game, and Silas stood to help gather the dishes.

"I've got this," she said when she saw him eyeing her dishwasher. "Just leave those on the counter."

He set the stacked plates on the counter as ordered but returned to the table to gather the rest.

"Lucy, ten minutes and then we head home."

"Okay."

"Thank you again," Carolina said, rinsing the plates before quickly loading the machine. "Lifting those display trays onto the golf cart is always the hardest part."

"Not a problem. Thanks for dinner. You're a better cook than I am. Lucy and I appreciated the invitation and not having to choke down my food or takeout again."

"Well, I hope it somehow made up for the problems I caused you earlier in the week." She loaded the last of the dishes with soap and shut the door with a flip of the lock. Done. Who said hyperactive people couldn't use their energy to their advantage? And this time she might not have forgotten anything since Silas gathered it all up.

She glanced at Silas and found him watching her. He smiled in response to getting caught in the act, and she liked the way it crinkled the little lines around his eyes.

"Carolina…"

She waited. And waited. "Yeah?"

Silas glanced over his shoulder at the kids and then back to her. "I'm sure you have plans for tomorrow with your family—"

"She doesn't," Samuel said from the couch.

"Thank you, Samuel." Way to make her sound like a loser.

"Don't forget I'm going to Tucker's house," Samuel continued.

"I remember." She hadn't, actually, but it was on the calendar and she would've checked, so it was kind of the same thing, wasn't it?

Carolina shifted her attention back to Silas and found him still staring at her. Her heart rate picked up speed. "Um, so, no, like Samuel said, I don't have plans. Frankie's going out with her biker friends, and London's is open and she's working. I always take the day off to finish prepping the bins on the golf cart, but now that you've attached them, all I have to do is fill them up tomorrow night before I head to the pier. Why do you ask?"

Silas inhaled and she got the feeling he was still on the fence about whatever it was he was about to say.

"Jake and Ann are going to the North End tomorrow for a cookout. A celebration for Mak before she leaves. Why don't you join us? It'll let me get to know you better and we can discuss the babysitting thing more."

Maybe hanging out wouldn't be so bad? Enough to get

the benefit of spending time with a good-looking man without, you know, the *benefits*? "Sounds fun."

"You'll go with us? Really?"

Lucy abruptly left the game and a grumbling Samuel behind to run into the kitchen, hands clasped in front of her in a pleading gesture.

Carolina nodded. "Of course. How could I resist this face?" Or his, she mused.

Chapter 11

People often said that even a bad day at the beach was still a day at the beach, and this July Fourth was definitely not a bad day. As he drove along the sand ruts to the end of the island, where Jake and Ann had set up for the day, Carolina laughed along with Lucy at the bumpy ride, and he found his mood improving even more. A sunny day, a beautiful woman, and Lucy's laughter. God bless America.

It didn't take long to find Jake's tricked-out truck and park. Jake's wife and teen girls had driven the truck to the North End of the island while Jake and his son had anchored their boat not far offshore. Now the older kids played on Jet Skis while Jake and his wife pitched in to unload Silas's truck.

While he set the base for the umbrella they'd need later, when the sun really began baking them, Silas watched as Carolina and Lucy finished setting up her chair before agreeing to go with Lucy to the water. Carolina had ditched her cutoffs and tank top and wore a modest red bikini that showcased her beautiful body to perfection. She'd left her long hair loose and curly, and the wind blew it along her shoulders and back, drawing his attention to wherever it landed.

"Now that's a pretty sight, my man," Jake said, lowering himself into one of the beach chairs.

Jake faced the surf, and even though there were probably fifty or so females in bathing suits in sight, Silas was aware of the niggle of jealousy he felt that Carolina had Jake's attention as well as that of other males nearby. "Where's your wife?"

"Right in front of me," he said, pointing to the water beyond Carolina. "Who'd you think I meant?"

Silas knew he'd been tricked because of the orneriness of Jake's grin. "Ann's just as curious as I am, though. When did you and Carolina become a thing?"

Silas gave the umbrella base one last twist and straightened. "We're not a thing."

"You sure about that? Because I heard your truck was at her house last night."

Ah, man. Carolina Cove might be crazy during tourist season, but when it was all said and done, it was a small town with nosy, too-observant neighbors. "Carolina helped me out by watching Lucy yesterday when school was canceled and Mak was shopping in Charlotte with Ann."

"I see. But why were you there so late?"

"Carolina needed help getting her golf cart ready for tonight so I helped her and… she made us dinner. What?"

"Nothing. But that sounds an awful lot like a *thing*, my man."

"Shut up and give me one of those."

Jake opened the cooler Silas had brought and tossed an icy can in Silas's direction, grinning unrepentantly.

"Want some advice?"

"What?"

"Don't screw it up."

"For the love of— There's nothing to screw up.

We're… friends. If today goes well, she might watch Luce for me until Mak gets back."

"Whatever. Just remember, if you date a Cohen sister, you date the whole family," Jake said, chuckling. "And that's a whole lotta estrogen."

OVER THE NEXT HOUR, they played in the water along the shore, baked in the sun, and talked about everything from current events to who had the best food in town. Around noon, Jake grilled steaks and chicken along with some veggies Ann had prepared, and Silas watched as Carolina dug into the second cooler to unearth the fruit, salads, and other stuff they'd picked up at the deli on the way.

Once their bellies were full, the sun blazed higher and hotter, and Lucy played under Jake and Ann's canopy with their youngest. Carolina watched the girls play tic-tac-toe with seashells before leaning back in her beach chair, eyes shaded as she stared at the water.

"Lucy is beautiful, inside and out."

He nodded his agreement and glanced back to check on his daughter. Jake's "surprise" child was two years younger than Lucy. The younger girl kept losing, and as Silas watched, his super-smart Lucy set her little friend up to win. "Thank you. I think so, too."

"I still can't believe she's so young and yet going to be in the same grade as Samuel. It blew my mind when she told me."

Silas inhaled and sighed, the sound heavy and deep to his own ears. "The summer program made a special allowance for her age so she could join in. The school hopes it'll help the transition this fall."

"I can't imagine testing out of a grade, much less multiple grades."

"Yeah, me either. I'm not sure it's a great idea for her socially to advance, especially since it's a new school for her, but I don't want to hold her back intellectually."

"I'm just amazed by her. My grades were passable on a good day."

She winced and shook her head, and Silas wondered at her thoughts. "What?"

"Nothing."

"Come on. You can't do that to me after I just fed you the ultimate steak."

"Mmm. That's true. What is it about eating out here by the water that makes everything taste that much better?"

She shoved herself upright in her chair and turned toward him, lowering her sunglasses down her nose so he got a good look at her eyes.

"The face is because I still feel so bad for ruining her first day of the program." She lowered her voice. "None of that would've happened if not for me cutting you off. I am *so* sorry. I promise I've learned my lesson. Won't happen again and I hope you won't hold it against me as far as whether or not you hire me to watch her."

Silas read the sincerity in Carolina's expression and nodded. "It's over. And if I've learned nothing else about Luce, it's that she's resilient. Once she calmed down, she was okay."

Carolina held his gaze a long moment before repositioning the sunglasses. "Good."

"I mean it. Staying with you yesterday was a huge step for a kid like her."

"A kid like her? Why do you say it like that?"

Silas didn't really want to bring down the mood by discussing such heavy details, but if he wound up hiring Carolina, she should probably know how things were with Lucy. "Lucy has a lot of anxiety," he said. "She's had panic attacks and issues ever since her mom left us."

"Oh."

Silas tried to judge Carolina's response but had a hard time because of the sunglasses.

"Um, how long ago was that?"

"Three years."

"She was a *baby*."

"Five. But, yeah, too young emotionally even though she was always ahead of the curve intellectually. She understood far more of what was happening than she was ready to handle."

"I remember Ireland—my sister—saying Sammy had nightmares after his dad left. It was really rough on them both, especially since his dad doesn't come around much. Dominic—Ireland's fiancé now—has done wonders for Sammy. Does Lucy's mom spend time with her? Contact her on birthdays? Christmas?"

Awkward conversations like this one were what made things hard. Finding that balance between how much to share and what to hold back. Baggage was baggage regardless of the weight. "No. In the package she left for us, Tara wrote she thought it would be best if she didn't see either of us."

"Package?"

"Yeah. A large envelope that contained divorce and custody papers she'd already signed, and a new book for Luce. We haven't heard from Tara since the day Lucy found her packing her bag."

Carolina stared in his direction for a long moment and he could only guess at her thoughts. Why had Tara left? Was it him? Something he'd done? What was so bad that a mother would abandon her child? Leave a marriage?

"I'm— Excuse me."

Silas watched as Carolina shot out of the chair toward the water and waded into the depths. He felt Jake's stare and look of concern at Carolina's abrupt departure, but he wasn't sure how to respond.

"Don't just sit there, doofus, go after her. We've got Lucy."

Silas got up and slowly walked across the sand, taking his time to try to formulate a conversation restarter since he'd screwed the last one up so badly. "Cooling off?"

"Oh, yeah."

He was taken aback by her tone, but even more than that, he was shocked when Carolina turned to face him and her chin trembled with emotion. "Whoa. What's wrong?"

She ducked down in the surf and walked backwards, away from the shore. "What's *wrong*? How can you not be angry twenty-four seven? It's bad enough she did that to you, but what kind of person does that to their kid? That sweet little girl"—her voice cracked but the wind carried the sound away—"is *so* precious. It's unthinkable to me that anyone could just pack a bag a-and walk away. Did you know she wanted to leave? Wanted a divorce?"

"No."

"Were you happy?"

"I thought we were. Carolina..." He took hold of her elbow and drew her to him when the waves forced them closer. They were chest deep now and he shifted his hands to her arms and up, over her shoulders to her neck, all the while telling himself to keep his hands off the potential sitter. "I told you so you'd understand if Lucy had a panic attack. It's about more than the moment. She's doing better now, but every now and again, when she's stressed, they still occur."

"I'm glad you told me. What your ex did to Lucy—to both of you... and what Rich did to my sister and Samuel... People *suck*."

She was furious on his behalf. On her sister's behalf.

And like it or not, her response drew him to her because when people heard the story, most of them shrugged and said that's just the way life was now, like changing partners equated to changing shampoos. "Carolina, that anger you feel is justified. It's good because it means you're a good person who hopes for the real kind of love."

"I don't know about that. I mean, what hope? To get my heart broken?"

"Are you that afraid of risk?"

"Aren't you?"

Jake's words about not letting Tara's betrayal keep him from finding someone came to mind. At least he and Carolina were in agreement when it came to this. "Whatever happens, the important thing is to get up again after we get knocked down. Your sister is engaged again, right?"

"Yeah, but what if Dominic does the same thing as Rich or your ex?"

"Then she'll get up again. It's not easy but it's what we have to do. Lucy, too."

"It's just so unfair. How are you so calm about it?"

He felt Jake and Ann watching their every move, so he gently steered Carolina a little deeper in the water between the shore and the sandbar farther out so that they could float and talk and look like the other couples playing and enjoying a beautiful day instead of discussing something as treacherous as life. "I wasn't. Not in the beginning—until I realized I had the one thing that mattered most and she needed me. Lucy wasn't okay. Her too-smart brain couldn't process what had happened. She was just starting to make progress with her therapist when the hurricane hit last year."

She was quiet a long time, floating. "I admire you, you know. You and Ireland. That you're still standing after all of that. And reasonably sane."

"Not too uptight?"

"Well..."

He grinned and lunged for her, pulled her back to his chest, and relished the feel of her against him as he braced them for a wave. "All things work for good—"

She lowered her head down his upper arm to see his face. "That's my mama's favorite verse."

"You look shocked that I know it."

"I kinda am."

He laughed at her honesty. "I'm no choirboy, it's true. Angry doesn't begin to describe how ticked off I was that everything bad kept happening *to me*. And all those church volunteers cycling through the area to help afterwards? I wanted to tell them where they could shove their benevolent spirit."

"So what changed?"

She relaxed in his arms and he began pulling her through the water toward the sandbar, her legs tangling with his every now and again. "Jake was a volunteer and we started talking. He offered me a job and told me to meet him at this house going up on the island. I took one look and I swear it was like the freaking thing mocked me."

"*Mocked you?* Why do you say that?"

They made it to where the sandbar canted up out of the water and half crawled out of the surf to plop down along the edge. He grabbed handfuls of wet sand and began making a dribble castle, as Lucy called them. "Because every beam and board in that house had a scripture written on it. Jake told me it had started with the owners writing on the boards every night after the crew left, to bless the house, but then the owners told the workers they could write their favorite verses too."

Carolina's lips parted in a smile. "I've heard of that house."

"A lot of locals have."

"So what happened?"

"Well, there I am, staring at all of these verses day in and day out. I'd lost everything. But I realized I had to make a choice. Stay down for the count or get up. Lucy tested out of her grade about the same time Jake found a rental on the island for us. It was a better school, great location. Timing-wise it all worked out like… it was meant to happen that way all along."

Carolina rolled onto her stomach and propped her chin on her folded arms. "Abandonment, divorce, a hurricane, a flooded house, and a new school. And it was *meant* to happen?"

"Why not?"

"I think the better question is why? I mean, I'm glad you can see it that way. I'm just not sure I'd be able to."

"Ah, that part is simple. You have to choose what you're going to believe. Is life against you or working out for you? Now that I've had some time to process things, I'm glad Tara left. It's better this way."

"Better?"

"I can't complain."

"Dude, you lost everything."

"Yeah." He reached out and nudged the sunglasses she'd worn into the water down her nose so he could see her beautiful eyes. "But look where I am now."

Chapter 12

"You need some sunscreen."

"Mmffpt," Carolina replied a half hour after wading back to their spot on the North End. She and Silas had built a dribble castle compound complete with moat and then splashed and played in the water. Now she lazed beneath the sun drying out, sleepy-cozy on a towel atop the soft sand.

"If you don't do it, I will. Can't have you burning."

"Mm."

"Is that an invitation?"

Was it? Her loose hair and folded arms hid her sleepy grin but she couldn't help herself. She liked this tough yet playful side of Silas. Their sandbar conversation had lowered some barriers and made her believe that maybe—just maybe—there were still some good guys out there.

She frowned at the thought just as Silas flipped the plastic cap of the sunscreen bottle. Seconds later, Silas's shiver-tastic hands smoothed over her neck and shoulders, and she couldn't stop the moan that emerged, even though it should've been a protest at the familiarity. Shouldn't it?

"Feel good?"

Oh, did it ever. Though she questioned the wisdom of giving him the privilege. Silas gently dug his thumbs into the muscles where she notoriously carried tension and took her breath away. She bit back a moan. Even her fingers dug into the sand but nothing could stop the pleasure sounds that escaped.

Silas's chuckle revealed his orneriness. He knew pressure points and wasn't afraid to manipulate them. And, boy, could he ever.

"Yo, Silas! We going or what?" Jake called.

She didn't want Silas to stop, but he needed some guy time and she needed to regain her muddled senses to ponder the surprising shift between them. "Mmm. Your boss is waiting."

"I'm not on the clock today."

"Mmm." *Oh, that felt so good!* "G-go. Have fun. I've got Lucy."

He eased the pressure with a lingering stroke down the center of her back before lightly swatting her behind. Yeah, not a boss-employee move at all. Was today turning into… more?

"Don't fall asleep and get burned. I'll be back in a bit to take you out on the water, okay?"

A nod was all she could muster after the goo-ish puddle he'd turned her into. And despite the urge to curl up and sleep as deeply as the sun-and-swim-tired Lucy did next to her, Carolina shoved herself up onto her elbows and turned to watch Silas don a life jacket as he entered the water near Jake's Jet Skis.

"Girl, you should see your face. That color's not from the sun."

Carolina laughed and dipped her head so her hair would hide her red cheeks.

"He likes you, you know."

Yeah, well, after the last couple of days, she liked him,

too. *Oh, Caro, what are you getting yourself into?* "He's... a nice guy."

"I'm glad you see that," Ann said, her gaze shifting to where the guys zipped along the shoreline. "I haven't seen Silas this relaxed since... ever. You're good for him."

Carolina rolled onto her side. "Well, that comes from the beautiful day."

"Maybe. Or from the fact he's enjoying himself with you."

"I am, too. Enjoying myself, that is. Thanks for the invitation."

"Sure, but... Carolina... go easy with them. Enjoying each other's company is fine, but they've both been through a lot."

She nodded, unable to do much else. "He told me."

"Really? Interesting," the woman said.

"What is?"

Ann shrugged but smiled. "Silas isn't much of a sharer."

"Carolina!"

She turned toward the water and saw Silas waving at her to come join him.

"There are extra vests in that bag there," Ann said, pointing. "I don't like the water, so you go ahead and have fun. I'll keep watch over Lucy."

"Are you sure?"

"Positive. Just remember what I said, okay? If you're not interested... don't let him think you are."

Seconds later Carolina climbed onto the back of the Jet Ski behind Silas and held tight as he idled out to deeper water before gunning the throttle. She laughed and squealed as they hopped the waves and bounced along the water, zigzagging across the area until Silas lifted his hand in Jake's direction and took off toward Masonboro Island.

Silas bypassed the popular spots where boats anchored

and people lazed about in the sun and kept going, finally slowing the motor and steering them toward an empty spot of sand. The area was devoid of people, and once they got to shallower depths, Silas cut the engine and they anchored the Jet Ski.

"Look!" She ran for the grass where the island canted upwards and carefully plucked up her treasure. "It's perfect! And no critter inside."

"Let me see."

She turned and found Silas right behind her, his words tickling her ear as he settled his forearm on one shoulder and grasped the hand holding the conch shell with the other. He shoved his sunglasses up his head and flipped the shell over to check the underside, examining it thoroughly.

"Looks like a great find."

"Thanks to you. I love coming out here but rarely get the chance."

"I thought you might like it. I heard you tell Luce you loved to shell hunt."

She tilted her head back and smiled up at him. She caught her breath, recognizing the look Silas wore. She might not have a lot of experience with men, but she knew when one wanted to kiss her. A thrill shot through her and she waited and, yeah, even secretly hoped. A second passed, two, and Silas lowered his head and brushed her lips with his. Sweet, gentle. Easygoing. He tasted her as though he had all the time in the world before gently turning her and pulling her closer to him.

The life jacket she wore made skin-to-skin contact impossible, but he deepened the kiss and she wrapped her arms around his neck, spread her fingers through his short hair, and shivered at the prickling sensation of it sliding over her skin.

Just when the world teetered and she didn't think she would ever breathe normally again, Silas lifted his head and ended the toe-curling kiss. Only then did she hear the catcalls and whistles hailing from a passing boat.

"We should go back."

"Five minutes." She smiled up at him and stripped off her life vest, revealing the red bikini beneath. "Best shell gets to drive us back?"

Silas's gaze swept over her and after a moment, he nodded.

"You're on."

Chapter 13

Silas lifted his hand and waved at Lucy as Carolina drove by on the brightly lit golf cart that night. The fireworks were about to start, and after several hours of driving back and forth with Lucy strapped into the passenger seat, Carolina's party wares could be seen blinking up and down the boardwalk.

He finished off the bottle of water he carried after a day of sweating in the heat and tossed it into the recycle bin, waiting for his girls to finish their final loop before parking. He might have known her all of a week, but Carolina had officially gotten under his skin. Now he wasn't sure how to proceed seeing as how dating his child-care worker could only end in disaster when—if—things went south.

But the smiles, the glances, their heavy conversation about his ex and Carolina's reaction to it, the way she played with Lucy… At some point he'd crossed the bridge of curiosity in regard to her energetic, free-spirited zaniness to something more. Lucy getting close to Carolina as a babysitter was one thing, but how wise was it to let Lucy get close if he wanted to date her? He straddled a fence and wasn't sure which side to land on.

He'd conceded the best shell win to Carolina but only because riding behind her on the Jet Ski meant he got to hold on to her curvy hips and small waist as she drove the Jet Ski as wildly as she drove her little Bug. Carolina exuded all that was fun, intriguing, and beautiful with a mix of southern charm and wit he found irresistible.

"The po-po are eyeing you because of how you keep staring at them."

"Wh—" Silas turned to find Jake grinning at him, and Officer Bobby Binet at Jake's side. "Oh, hey, Bobby. Didn't see you walk up."

"So I noticed. Do I need to be concerned Carolina's stalker fears are true?" Bobby asked, struggling to maintain his serious expression.

"Nah," Jake said. "Spotted them kissing earlier so I think they've come to terms. Right, Silas?"

Silas ignored Jake's sly grin and took the ribbing in stride. "Don't you two have better things to do than give me a hard time?"

Jake and Bobby looked at each other before shrugging and shaking their heads. "Nope," they said in unison.

They made small talk and waited until Carolina and Lucy pulled the cart up to the pier house and out of the way minutes before the fireworks began.

Spectators *oohed* and *ahhed* with every colorful burst, and he plopped Lucy atop his shoulders for a better view above the crowd. Carolina made more sales as the show took place, and by the time the grand finale lit up the sky, only a few trinkets and toys remained.

Carolina drove them back to Holland's house, where he'd left his truck. Lucy crashed during the short ride, and Silas plucked her from between him and Carolina and carried his daughter to the truck.

She stirred as he strapped her into her booster seat. "Daddy?"

"Yeah, baby."

"Today was the best day ever," Lucy said without opening her eyes. "Will Carolina keep me?"

Maybe it was the way Lucy worded her question but Silas felt his heart crack at the pain it brought. Lucy came first. Always. And so did Lucy's happiness. "I'll ask." He kissed her cheek and left the truck to find Carolina waiting nearby. "You get the cart locked up?"

"Yes. Silas… thank you. For today, and helping with the cart."

"You're welcome," he said, shoving his hands into his pockets to keep from doing what he wanted to do, which was tug her close and kiss her again to see if it blew his mind as much as the first kiss had. If she didn't take the job, he could do just that. But if she did… "Are you still interested in babysitting Lucy?"

"Oh, yes. Absolutely."

Disappointment filled him, but he reminded himself that it was two weeks, and maybe it was time he needed to get his headspace straight. "Mak leaves Monday. I thought about what you said about watching her at the inn and coffeehouse. If you can change your schedule for the duration, I'll be okay with that."

"Consider it done."

"Okay. Well, I should get Lucy home."

Carolina took a step forward as Silas stepped back and he caught a flash of hurt surprise on her features. "Carolina… about today and what happened. If you're going to be Lucy's babysitter, I don't think we should… I mean, maybe it would be best if we didn't muddy the water, you know? At least while Mak is gone."

"Oh. Oh, of course. I-I totally understand. Today… It was… Yeah, I get it. I-I agree. Of course."

He inhaled and the sea breeze carried the alluring scent of her perfume. He wanted to kiss her again. Ached to. In two weeks' time, maybe he would.

"I'll text you my schedule so you know where to pick her up," Carolina said.

"Thanks. Good night, Carolina. I'll… see you Monday evening."

Chapter 14

The next two weeks crawled by in a haze of awkwardness, because with every Lucy pickup Silas performed, he acted as though he hadn't kissed Carolina thoroughly enough to make her toes curl in the sand. And while she wanted to talk things over with her sisters to get their take, she couldn't. Not when it meant opening herself up to their criticism because *why* would she want things with Silas to be more when she planned to leave town to travel once the season was over?

Finally the last day of babysitting arrived. Lucy was currently curled up in the break room behind the desk at the inn, and Carolina stood nose deep in the spare linen closet, restocking extra sheets, toiletries, and the like for after-hours housekeeping requests.

"That was an awfully heavy-sounding sigh."

Silas.

Carolina momentarily froze before lifting her chin and pinning a smile to her face. She tucked the tag of a towel beneath the material on the shelf and then firmly shut the door after snagging a roll of paper towels to hold on to because she needed something to do with her hands. "Hey. How was work?"

Inane, stupid question. But she always asked and he always said—

"Good. Glad to be home with my baby girl, though."

Yeah, that.

"Lucy asked me last night if you could babysit her after school or weekends when Mak isn't able to. Sort of a backup plan from now on. I told her I'd ask."

She stared up at him. Took in the dark, dark tan he had from being in the sun so much and the way it made his eyes practically glow. "Oh, um… yeah, she mentioned it, too, but I don't think I can. I mean, I'd love to. Lucy is wonderful and certainly not any trouble, but I'm looking for another side hustle so it's unlikely I'll be available."

That wasn't the real reason. It was a reason, sure, but the real reason was that she'd had a really hard time the last two weeks liking a man who only looked at her like a babysitter, and she didn't want to be on pins and needles every time she got a call or a text from him because he wanted her to keep his precocious kid. Mak was dating age. What were the odds that if she agreed to be the backup, Silas would eventually call her to keep Lucy because *he* was going out that night as well? No. Nope. Nada. Not doing it. "Sorr—"

She wasn't sure how it happened. She couldn't quite make eye contact during her heavily prepared speech, so she didn't see him move toward her. Didn't know he'd lowered his head while at the same time fitting a hand under her chin to lift it. His lips brushed hers before lifting and she gaped up at him. "What… What was that for?"

"Turning me down."

"Okay. I'm… confused."

"Carolina, I'm smart enough to know I can't kiss Lucy's babysitter. Not without risking Lucy getting hurt."

His gaze lowered to her lips and her heart rate soared.

"But since you've officially turned down the job…"

"That makes me kissable?" Dang, those little crinkles around his eyes were sexy when he smiled.

"Yeah. It does."

She'd felt his and Lucy's desperation in needing help during Mak's absence, but looking at him now, she kind of wished she'd said no two weeks ago.

"What are you doing tonight? Aren't you getting off work soon?"

She swallowed hard and nodded. "Six."

"Can I pick you up at seven?"

"As in a date?"

"Yes."

The question practically scrambled her brain. To give herself a moment to think and deal with the scattershot of her thoughts, she asked, "Do you have childcare?"

He chuckled at her question and slid his hand along her jawline to tuck her hair over her shoulder. "Mak is on standby. Since I was near the airport earlier, I offered to pick her up and she said she's anxious to earn some cash since she blew a lot of her savings on the trip. I told her I'd let her know if I was going out."

"And if I'd agreed to watch Lucy for you in the future?"

"I wouldn't have asked."

Wow. The man had some serious boundaries. Good to know.

"So, what do you say? Will you go out with me?"

His thumb brushed over her lower lip and she realized she'd bitten it to the point of pain. Should she do this? Go? She definitely wanted to but what if… "I'll be ready at seven."

· · ·

EVENING ARRIVED and Carolina's room looked like a tornado had blown through before swirling back around for a second performance.

Carolina stared at the utter chaos of her clothes and shoes and bags and dresses and wanted to scream. She'd picked out the perfect outfit for her date with Silas, but when she'd put it on, she'd smudged makeup on her blouse, which meant changing. And changing. And changing. Now she was still in her underwear—and locked in panic-mode because she'd heard Silas's voice downstairs five minutes ago.

"Caro? Hey, your date is wai— wow," Holland drawled after she poked her head inside of the bedroom. "Look out, Hurricane Caro."

Carolina turned and something about her expression must have registered the depth of her panic, because Holland quickly ducked inside the door and shut it behind her.

"Take a breath."

"I can't. Tell him I can't go."

"What? He's *here*. Caro, you went out with him on the Fourth and you said it was fun."

"Yeah, it was up until he said he couldn't date me."

"Why was that?"

"Because of Lucy. Silas didn't think it would be a good idea to go out if I was her babysitter."

"Okay, wow, again. I really wanted to not like the guy after the not-date-you comment because I thought maybe he was stringing you along, but that's… admirable."

"I *know*."

"So, if you admire him, what's the problem? Why the drama?"

The drama was because just when she didn't think she could like Silas more, he went and upped his likeableness. Most men were horndogs who'd do whatever to whomever whenever they could get away with it, but Silas had not only set boundaries to protect his kid, the last two weeks he'd proved to her that he was a man of his word by sticking to them.

It wasn't the date that made it different. It was the man. But she couldn't say that. Because saying it out loud meant she already knew she was in over her head where Silas was concerned and *that*?

That terrified her even more. Who felt like this in such a short amount of time? It was weird. It was a disaster waiting to happen. It was… lust?

Holland moved over as though to sit on the side of the bed, but there were so many clothes thrown atop it, she changed directions mid-stride and headed for the bench in front of the window. There, she shoved a half-dozen purses onto the floor.

"Hey. You're making more of a mess."

Holland's expression could only be described as sardonic.

"Like that's possible in here. Now, come on. What's going on?"

"I don't know." How could she explain her fears to someone as sophisticated and worldly as Holland? Because even though she had a substantial amount of attraction for Silas, she couldn't label what she felt as strictly lust. She just knew it couldn't be love and wasn't sure what the middle-ground term was when it came down to "it."

"Ha. You never could pull that with me. Fine. Don't tell me, but I'll find out. You know I will."

"Holland, *help me*." She spread her arms to indicate the colorful array discarded in anxiety-thrown tosses. "I have nothing to wear."

"Seriously? Carolina, what's gotten into you? Why are you so wigged out about this?"

"I don't know," she repeated. But even as the words

came out of her mouth, she knew they both knew the statement was a lie.

"Amazing."

"What?"

"You. I've never seen you like this. You *really* like him, don't you?"

She met her sister's gaze but couldn't form an answer… but wasn't that an answer in itself? "He's… a good kisser."

"Okay. And?"

"And… my freaking toes curled when he kissed me."

"Dang."

"I know, right? But— But— But—"

"*Buuut?*"

"Do I *want* that?"

"Um, I'm pretty sure *all* women want that. With the right person, I mean." Holland's gaze narrowed. "Are you worried he's *not* the right person? Did he say or do something that sent up a red flag?"

Carolina thought hard but… "No."

"Caro, you seriously have to take a breath. It's just nerves."

She winced. "You're not helping me."

"Look, you obviously hit it off with Silas and it's rattled you. But there's nothing to be scared of," Holland said, lowering her voice to match Carolina's softer tone after Carolina frantically waved her hands in the air and motioned for her to be quieter.

She was so scared Silas might hear her. Not what she needed right now!

"Says you."

"Fine. You know what, don't go."

"What? But—"

"But nothing. You agreed earlier but now your gut is obviously telling you not to go, so don't."

"But he's such a nice guy. And I want to go, it's just… Dang it, Holland, I hate it when you use reverse psychology on me."

Holland grinned. "Works every time, too. That's the amazing thing."

Carolina picked up a pillow and threw it at her.

Holland caught it and tossed the pillow aside. "No one says there has to be another date, you know. So go, enjoy if you can, and if not, there's your answer."

She inhaled and held the breath in an attempt to slow her racing heart. "Right. Of course. I'm projecting. Worrying about something that might not be an issue. He could say something tonight that would be a total turnoff, right? What am I thinking? Of course." She plucked up a bright pink sundress. "It's dinner. No big deal."

"That's right. But that's not the dress. Try that one." Holland waggled a finger toward a dress she'd given Carolina for her birthday.

"Really?"

"It's perfect for where he's taking you. Put it on."

She pulled it over her strapless bra and underwear and twisted and turned to try to reach the zipper.

"Turn. I got you."

"Are you sure a dress isn't too much? What about shorts? Wait, you know where we're going? He told me it was a surprise."

"Can we focus here? The dress is elegant and sexy but not overdone. And it looks great on you. Trust me."

"But—"

"He's waiting, Caro, and… he may have mentioned something about reservations."

"Reservations?" She gulped. Did Silas have the money for that kind of thing as a single dad? As someone who'd lost everything?

And while he was making reservations, here she was

second-guessing her acceptance of the date. How awful was that?

And the award for the Worst Date Ever goes to…

"Don't panic. That just means *this* is the dress. Now, turn."

Holland's hands settled on Carolina's shoulders and her sister flipped her around with dizzying speed.

"Perfect. Spritz some perfume, grab some shoes, and you're good to go."

"But—"

"Caro, stop. He made your toes curl and it scared you. I get it. But maybe it was a fluke."

Carolina stared at her sister. Maybe it *was* a fluke. Maybe the next kiss wouldn't curl anything and that… would be a good thing. Then all of the fear and anxiety she felt due to the potential decisions she'd have to make between the plans she had to travel and the guilt she'd feel leaving Silas and Lucy would be a moot point.

But they'd discussed her plans to travel while working on the golf cart, and Silas had asked her out anyway, so see? *You are stressing for nothing!*

Holland tilted her beautiful blond head to one side, her confusion changing to dawning understanding.

"Wait a minute… Caro, what aren't you saying?"

"Nothing."

"Liar."

"It's just… Silas is great. But not liking him would keep things simple."

"What things? Simple how?"

Oh, no. She wasn't going to go down that rabbit hole. Her family didn't like her grand idea of traveling the world as a house sitter. Holland especially. She shrugged and avoided her sister's gaze. "Nothing. I have to go."

Holland's expression revealed her suspicious thoughts, but after a glance at her fancy watch that probably cost more than Carolina made in a year working three jobs—which reminded her of her goals and dreams of worldwide travel—Holland shooed Carolina over to the pile of shoes lying on the floor outside of the closet.

"Wear those wedges. Yeah, those."

Carolina grabbed them and leaned her rear against the dresser for balance while she put them on. When she straightened, Holland waited with a perfume bottle at the ready.

"Hold your breath."

Holland spritzed her as Carolina twirled to get the full effect. Time to go greet her date.

"Wait."

Carolina frowned because of the seriousness of Holland's expression. "What? Do I look okay?"

"You look great. Just… don't laugh."

"O-kay." Don't laugh?

"I mean it, Caro. Listen to what I'm about to say."

A knot formed in her stomach but she nodded. "Okay, sure."

"You've made quite a few comments about my life and dating over the years, and I'll admit it's been pretty amazing at times."

Like she needed *that* reminder?

"But… the thing is, I've never had a man make my toes curl."

Carolina's eyes widened. Seriously? With all of the rich, gorgeous hotties Holland had dined with over the years working a job most people would kill to have… "*Never?*"

"Never. I've been wined and dined in some of the most beautiful places in the world, but the whole time I was there? There was this… emptiness that I couldn't shake. Don't get me wrong. They were great guys. Just not the guys for me."

"But your life is so glamorous and exciting."

"At times. And at times it's nothing but delayed planes and deadlines and stress, just like any other job." Holland shrugged and laughed, though the sound was decidedly uncomfortable. "I'm not saying I haven't had fun. I've met some great people. Been kissed plenty of times. Some of the men have been intriguing but… none of them have ever had that li'l bit of something that made me wonder if I should stay longer or… hope there could be more."

Oh, hold up there. "I never said it could be more with Silas."

"You didn't have to, but my instincts are telling me that's why you're in such a panic."

Carolina inhaled and tried to calm the surge inside of her. Her emotions seemed even more raw and exposed due to her sister's insight.

She couldn't deny the anxiety she felt, but was that really it, though? Did she feel that Silas just might possess that "li'l bit of something" that had her thinking of her dreams and plans and wondering how they'd ever mesh. "It's too soon," she repeated. "We barely know each other."

"And Mama says when it's right, we'll know it. Look, I'm not saying he is or isn't. You're the only one who knows that. But don't be in such a hurry to back away from something out of fear."

Fear. Was she backpedaling out of fear—or simply focusing on dreams yet to come true?

Chapter 15

Carolina wasn't sure what to expect, but driving to the marina at the state park instead of traveling 421 was a pretty good start. She loved being on the water. Loved the salt air in her lungs and wind in her hair. And floating along the Cape Fear River was way better than battling the bustling summer traffic to Wilmington.

The sun sank lower in the sky as Silas captained Jake's boat toward downtown. She liked that he didn't push the boat to its limits just because he could. Silas was respectful with his friend and boss's possession. Yet another thing to admire, not that she needed more.

She'd watched a lot of men captain boats over the years. Nearly all of them had floored the gas and gone for speed, zipping along the shore too fast to enjoy the experience.

Silas was one of the few exceptions, and as she sat behind the protective windshield and they trolled along at a steady pace, she felt another barrier lower as he pointed out birds, animals, boats, and other sights he thought she might enjoy.

Carolina helped Silas tie up to a restaurant's floating dock, and once secure, Silas held out his hand to help her. He pulled her close in the process, and there was no mistaking the interest in his gaze as he stared down at her.

"Have I told you how beautiful you look?"

She wasn't a vain person. She didn't always have to have makeup on or be dressed just right, but she was feminine enough, and admittedly needy enough, that having Silas tell her she was beautiful gave her more than a few tingles. "Thank you. You clean up pretty good yourself."

In typical coastal local fashion, he'd worn khakis paired with a salmon-colored shirt that brought out his tan and the blue of his eyes. The breeze carried his cologne to her nose, and she inhaled appreciatively, taking in the spice and man and something... woodsy. When she thought about the first time she'd met him face to... well, chest and now, she couldn't help but smile. Some men slathered cologne on to the point of suffocating those around them, but once again, Silas had gone for a more low-key approach. Yet another thing to like.

Carolina caught her breath, only then realizing she'd stood there staring up at him for several long moments. Silas lowered his head and brushed his lips over her forehead before stepping away and using his hold on her hand to tug her toward the river entrance of the restaurant.

"Just in time," he murmured as they approached the hostess. They were quickly shown to their table by the windows and Silas held her chair while she settled in.

"I can't believe you were able to get a reservation on such short notice." Silas shrugged but something didn't seem right. "When did you call?"

He inhaled and released an uncomfortable-sounding chuckle. "Honestly? Two weeks ago."

But that meant—

"I hoped you'd say no to babysitting once Mak returned so… What can I say? I'm an optimist."

A sweet, thoughtful, handsome optimist, which made her fear level ratchet up another fifty notches.

Dinner became a contest to see who could tell the most outrageous true story. Silas drew from his experiences as a single dad and things he'd seen working as a contractor, and she pulled from her deep well of sisterly antics. They ate and talked and laughed the entire time, and she didn't remember ever enjoying a man's company as much as this.

"Sweetheart, you win," he said, smiling at her from across the table. "I can't believe y'all put your poor father through that. The man deserves a medal."

Mmm. Some snobby people might look down on southern accents, but Carolina had a soft spot for them, and Silas's low drawl sent tingles down her spine. His deep, rich voice made her wonder if he could sing. "Just because we used to sneak out?"

"Sneaking out times the *five* of you. It's enough to make a man's heart give out. I only have Lucy to look out for at this point, but I'm thinking I should lock her away in a bunker somewhere until she's at least thirty-five."

"Well, Daddy never would've known had we not gotten stuck and *had* to call him, but when he got stuck and had to call the tow truck…"

"From what I can tell, occasionally getting stuck is a normal thing for an *experienced* driver on the sand. Ireland barely had her license."

"Whatever. We would've been fine except Chewy showed up. That's what sent Dad and the tow truck driver over the edge."

He shook his head at her, a handsome smile curling his lips. "You're lucky *Chewy* didn't chew on *you* and chose to chomp a tire instead. You girls were blessed to get out of there without losing a limb."

She might have exaggerated the danger of the story just a tad to win the contest, but she also knew a baby alligator wasn't anything to sneeze at. They finished dinner and she excused herself to go to the ladies' room, and Carolina returned as their waitress brought the bill.

"Thank you," he said, handing the woman some cash. "Keep it."

"Thank you. Have a great rest of your evening."

Carolina saw the waitress smile at Silas and, before she could stop it, a feeling of inadequacy arose. With four siblings, she'd been privy to a lot of relationship battles and woes over the years. Boyfriends and fiancés and even a husband—Ireland's first—who'd lied and cheated, which meant she'd walked with them through a few broken hearts. Was this fated to be one for her? What was she doing here?

"Hey. Are you ready to get back out there?" Silas asked when he spotted her.

The waitress turned to see who Silas spoke to and Carolina forced a bright smile. "Absolutely. That sunset is going to be amazing." Carolina tried her best to shrug off her feelings. Her mama always said feelings couldn't be trusted. And truthfully? She couldn't have it both ways. She couldn't want whatever future toe-curls Silas *might* represent while at the same time *not* want what that relationship would require from her. That one-sided teeter-totter would be doomed to failure.

How did she get herself into this mess? Was she really that easily swayed by blue eyes and tanned muscles?

"Carolina? Is something wrong?"

She blinked to awareness and realized Silas had stood and now waited for her to move toward the exit, but she'd gone off into La-la Land. *Focus.* "No. Sorry. Daydreaming."

"About?"

She faltered beneath his quizzical stare and managed a smile. "Just wondering if winning the contest means I get to captain Jake's boat on the way back."

Chapter 16

A half hour later, Silas stood behind Carolina as they slowly motored back to where he'd parked his truck.

The air was warm but humid, and bombed with the breeze, she shivered. Silas moved his hands from her waist to her bare arms and lightly smoothed them down to her elbows and back up again. If he hadn't been watching her so closely, he might've missed the way her teeth sank into her lower lip and how she inhaled a shaky breath. Carolina rested more of her weight against his chest, and he wrapped his arms around her to share his body heat. "You're a natural at this."

The words must have tickled her ear because she shivered once again. Carolina might be a whirlwind of color and chaos, but she didn't hide her reactions well and he liked that. "Sensitive, aren't you?"

He trailed his lips over her earlobe, down to her neck, where he nibbled. Her grip on the wheel tightened and she tilted her head to one side.

"Y-you want me to crash us?"

He couldn't stop the chuckle that formed. "Definitely not. Are you having fun?"

She nodded quickly, a smile on her lips. "Yeah. Yeah, I am. You?"

"Best night I've had in a long time."

The sun had set and her beautiful blue eyes sparkled as they they made their way around the curve in the island, back to the marina. Visibility was good despite the waning light, and he knew they'd get there just in time, though the night was still early.

Once they approached the dock, Silas took the wheel and maneuvered the boat into Jake's slip. In a matter of minutes, they walked hand in hand to his truck, and he second-guessed his plans for the rest of the evening.

Would someone like Carolina think him too boring? Not exciting enough? First impressions being what they were, he could see her dancing the night away in Wilmington, whereas he tended to be a homebody. He could blame the tendency on Lucy, but he wasn't a partier and preferred a boat ride at sunset with a beautiful woman over a smelly, sweaty group of strangers and too loud music.

He helped her into the truck and climbed in beside her but paused to look at her before shifting it into gear. "Since it's early still, I thought maybe we'd go for a walk on the beach. But if that's too boring—"

"It's perfect. I'd love that."

"Yeah?" He liked her smile. Liked her.

"When I'm near the beach, I'm usually working, so just going to walk and hang out sounds great."

He nodded once. "Let's get going then."

Parking anywhere near the pier got tricky this time of year, but Silas managed to snag a spot toward the end of the pavilion parking.

Carolina had opened her door by the time he made it around the large truck, but instead of getting out, he saw her working to remove her shoes. "Ah. Sorry. Didn't think of that." Which just proved how out of practice he was when it came to this sort of thing.

"Not a problem. Beach life, right?"

She'd unbuckled one shoe and he lightly grasped her ankle in his hand to help with the other, removing it about the same time as she dropped the first to the floor of his truck.

"Let me." He scooped her up and grinned at her laughing shriek of surprise. "Can't have you getting a splinter. Get the door?"

Carolina wrapped one arm around his neck and shut the door with the other. Her perfume teased him as he carried her across the weathered boardwalk to one of the beach access points. About halfway down the walkway, the boards were covered in sand no doubt washed ashore during the hurricane that had brought so much change to his life.

"Are you going to carry me the whole way?"

The breathless quality of her voice called to something deep inside of him. "I might. Afraid I'll drop you?"

He hefted her into the air a bit just to catch her again and liked how she clung to him, laughing all the while.

"Not a bit. I've watched you working with your crew."

Silas glanced down at her and paused. Carolina had tilted her head back and stared up at him. The ocean breeze blew her loose hair along the arm supporting her back, teasing him. With the full moon overhead, the waves crashing along the shore, and Carolina in his arms, he felt… content. "You have, huh?"

As she realized she'd been caught in her words, her lashes fell low over her eyes and her teeth sank into her lower lip. The sight of it made him want to follow and see how good she'd taste after their dessert at the restaurant.

"Get a room!" someone called from the boardwalk. Laughter followed the teenager's call.

"Oh, geez."

Silas chuckled at her embarrassed murmur and reluctantly lowered her to her feet.

"Thanks for… saving me from splinters."

Silas kept his arm around her back and, despite the intense urge to kiss her, managed not to. A few deep breaths cleared the thoughts he'd had while holding her against him and hammered home the fact he missed being with a woman. He missed having a companion. The laughter and shared experiences, conversation. And, of course, the physical contact being in a relationship brought. The touching, holding. Kissing. Sex.

He hadn't had much time to date in the last year or so, and when his first attempts had gone so badly, he hadn't had any interest. He told himself it was because he was so busy trying to rebuild a life for Lucy, but truth be told, he hadn't found a woman intriguing enough to make it worth the effort. The time he'd spent with Carolina this last week had brought that desire back to life.

They walked a bit from the walkway before he toed off his comfortable shoes, and they continued on toward the surf in silence. The beach held a variety of visitors. Fishermen handled multiple poles along the shore, and families wielded flashlights as they searched for crabs and shells. Farther back against the dunes, couples sat talking or making out where it was darker, more private.

In sync, they headed toward the pier and walked beneath the massive pilings. In the shadows beneath, Silas pulled Carolina close to his side and wrapped his arm around her shoulders, liking the way she fit against him.

Maybe Jake was right about what he'd said about dating.

Step by step, life proved to be more fun with this Carolina girl around.

Chapter 17

Carolina stared into her coffee the following Sunday morning, lost to the haze of her thoughts and the confusion she felt after last night had ended in a make-out session. Two dates in two days, both of which had involved toe-curling kisses.

"Hello? Earth to Caro. Are you ready?"

She blinked to awareness and turned to find Holland and Samuel both staring at her. "Huh?"

Holland's gaze narrowed.

"You're acting weird, Aunt Caro," Samuel informed her. "Even for you."

"Gee, thanks, kid."

Holland gave Carolina a shrewd-eyed *oh yeah* glance and waved a hand for the door. Samuel had raced out of the house to snag the front seat of the golf cart even though he knew she'd order him to the rear like every other time he'd done it in the past. Somehow it had become part of their Sunday morning routine when Holland or Ireland would cart to church and give her a ride to work at the same time.

Carolina slid off of the island barstool and smoothed a

hand over her shorts and Carolina Cove Inn T-shirt. Beach church was just that, near the beach, and come as you are, so there was a wide variety of outfits, from dresses and shorts typically worn by the locals to bathing suits and cover-ups worn by visitors heading to the beach once the service was over.

"You've avoided me since Friday and don't think I don't realize why. I *will* get a full report before the day is over," Holland said as she held the door for Carolina to exit.

"There's not a lot to say."

Carolina had only just made it to the threshold when her sister quickly pressed an arm across to the other side, barring exit.

"Was there toe-curling?"

"You really think this is an appropriate conversation before church?"

Holland raised her eyebrows high and waited.

"Okay, fine. Yeah. There was definite... curling."

Holland grinned but didn't remove the arm stopping Carolina's progress through the door.

"And?"

"And... it was great. It was awesome, but—"

"But *what*? Are you back to worrying about what might or might not happen tomorrow or next week or next year? Because you can't do that to yourself."

"I know. Okay? I know, but at some point, when you're making plans, you need a clue about what you're doing. I'd think you of all people would understand."

"I do."

"Do you? Because you're starting to sound like Mama and Daddy. I want to do things and go places, and a relationship changes... *every*thing."

"Wait, so you haven't talked about your plans?"

"Not since before the toe-curling, no."

"I see. Well, normally I'd say there's no rush but, Caro,

if you really aren't interested, don't play games with the guy. That's just mean."

"I'm not playing games. I'm just… Silas knows I work like crazy just so I can travel in the off-season."

"So he does know."

"That I like to travel? Yeah."

"Then maybe you need to stop thinking so much and just let things play out as they're meant to."

"You sound like Silas. He says things work the way they're supposed to, but how are my travel plans going to work with him and Lucy?"

"Caro, maybe that's the point."

"What?"

Holland gave Carolina that older-sister, I-know-more-than-you-do stare.

"That you're not supposed to know how it'll work, just trust that it will."

"But—"

"Hey, you call me and Ireland control freaks all the time, but who's sounding like one now?"

"Hello! Mom and Dominic are already there! Are we going?" Samuel called from the driveway.

"Caro?"

"Forget it."

"You realize you're self-sabotaging, right? Worrying about stuff that may or may not happen? Why does Silas freak you out so much?"

Oh, such a good question. Carolina stared into Holland's gaze and wondered how and *why* her sister had such an insight into the way her brain worked. "I'm just being cautious, okay? All y'all say I'm too impetuous and make decisions too quickly. Now I'm a control freak? Maybe I just don't want to screw up." Hard stomps headed up the stairs toward them. "We're going to be late. We'd better corral him while we can."

Holland lowered her hand and Carolina quickly ducked through and met Samuel at the top of the stairs. "Hold up. We're coming."

"What's taking so long?"

"We had to grab purses," she said by way of an excuse that didn't involve lying.

"*Girls*," Samuel said in disgust.

SILAS MET Jake and his family at the pavilion before beach church and thanked Mak again for watching Lucy last night. When he'd gone to their house to pick Lucy up, his daughter had already fallen asleep, so Ann insisted Lucy stay put. Jake's wife had ordered Silas home to get some sleep. And even though he felt bad because Lucy was his responsibility, he knew not to turn down the offer.

Holland, Carolina, and Samuel rolled by on the golf cart, looking for a parking space.

"Daddy, can I go say hi to Carolina? I miss her."

Apparently he wasn't the only one who'd noticed.

"You should tell her," Jake said, grinning widely at Silas. "Your daddy will take you."

Silas shook his head at Jake's comment but nodded at Luce. "Let's hurry before the service starts."

By the time Holland found a parking spot, Silas and Lucy were within talking distance. He watched as Carolina exited the cart and caught her look of surprise when she spotted him.

"Um, hi."

"Hi, Carolina."

Carolina tilted her head and smiled at his little girl, and despite the unreadable expression she'd worn seconds earlier, Carolina seemed genuinely happy to see Lucy.

"Hey, you. I've missed you."

"I've missed you, too. Are you coming to church with us?"

"You do have plenty of time to attend before your shift starts," Holland interjected. "Hi, Silas. Who's this?"

"I'm Lucy."

"Well, hello, Lucy. It's nice to meet you. I'm Carolina's sister Holland. I hear you're in Samuel's class?"

"Yeah. It's so much fun."

Silas smiled when he caught Samuel rolling his eyes.

"Have you decided on your project yet for the program?" Carolina asked.

"Yes. But the teacher says I have to have a partner and I can't start until I do."

Silas watched as both Carolina and Holland turned to find Samuel staring at his feet.

"Who's your partner, Sammy? Anyone we know?" Holland asked.

"Don't have one yet. But—"

"Will you be my partner? I want to monitor the change in tides," Lucy said, blinking up at Samuel from behind her glasses.

Silas almost felt sorry for the kid because of the pressure he was under to say yes given the way all three females stared at him, but Samuel surprised Silas by immediately shrugging.

"I guess. Doesn't matter much to me."

It wasn't the most thrilled response, but Lucy didn't seem to notice.

"Good. Maybe you and Silas can get them together this week and give Ireland a chance to catch up from her trip," Holland said, sounding very motherly.

"Sounds like a plan," Silas said, nodding at the kids. He couldn't think of anything better than walking along the beach with Carolina.

"Come on, kids. Let's go score some seats. See you two in a few minutes."

Holland smiled at him and Carolina, and he wondered at the expression on her face. "You okay?"

"What? Oh, yes. I'm good."

He took a step closer. "Is it bad that I'd really like to kiss you good morning?" He glanced at the pavilion and found Jake and Ann unabashedly watching their every move, along with several other parishioners.

"Probably not any worse than me wanting you to."

He took another step closer, but instead of kissing her lips like he wanted, he reached out and clasped her hand in his, linking their fingers and lifting hers to his lips. He kissed her hand before tucking it close to his chest. "What am I going to do with you, Miss Cohen?"

Carolina flashed him a saucy smile. "I have a few ideas."

"Is that right?"

"Yeah, let's go," she said, using her hold to tug him down the boardwalk as though heading toward the inn before she quickly cut across the road to the pavilion and church.

Silas chuckled as he followed her, imagining the day he'd lead her to church for a whole other reason.

Chapter 18

Carolina cleaned off the table at London's Lattes and lifted the tray to carry back to the bar. Not long after London had met Rocco's master, her sister had asked Carolina to pick up more evenings every week. Fast-forward to now and Carolina knew by the end of the season she'd have enough for a few extra stops along whichever destination route she decided upon.

The door jingled as it opened and she looked up to find her parents entering. "Hey! You're back. How was the trip?"

"Beautiful," her mother said.

"Another one for the memory books," her dad added. "What's going on here?"

"Not much, as you can see. Why do tourists always seem to come in waves?"

"Always happens that way," he father said. "I think they start to mimic the tides."

She laughed at the joke and leaned against the counter-top. "Can I get you anything?"

"Surprise me," Andrea said, taking a seat at one of the high-top tables.

"Ooh, Mama's living on the edge."

"Nothing for me, hon, thanks."

"Your father and I heard you've been busy while we've been gone. Dates with a friend of Jake McMurphy?"

Carolina snagged the ingredients to make her mother's surprise coffee and shrugged. "Well, that didn't take long. It's no big deal, Mama."

"Oh."

Carolina lifted her eyebrows at her mother's tone and inhaled before she braved crossing the floor to where they sat. "Stop it. I mean it."

"But you're young and beautiful. You deserve a good man and I have it on good authority—"

"Isn't gossiping bad?"

"Carolina Rose, you stop that right now. We just want you to be happy."

"Who says I'm not?" She lowered the mug onto the table in front of her mother. "Mama, just because I'm not a mother at twenty-five like you were doesn't mean I'm not happy."

"But maybe you wouldn't go on those crazy trips all alone if you met—"

"Stop, stop, stop. Daddy, help me out here," she said, looping her arm over her father's shoulders. She leaned against his side and pressed a kiss to his bald head. "You understand, don't you?"

Her father squeezed her waist and hugged her close.

"That I do, baby girl. But there's nothing that says you can't have roots and wings."

She leaned her head back and groaned. "Okay, next subject. Tell me about your crazy trip. What did you do? What did you see?"

Andrea wagged a finger in Carolina's direction.

"This conversation isn't over."

Carolina inhaled and sighed deeply. "Yes, Mama."

AUGUST ARRIVED and with it school started up again. Between working, juggling Lucy's schedule, and seeing Carolina nearly every single day, Silas dropped into bed at night exhausted but happy.

Still, something had to give. And soon. He knew how he felt about Carolina, and the urge to tell her he loved her grew stronger with every day that passed. But he also didn't want to be the first one to say it. Wasn't that a female thing? Weren't women the ones who always said that first?

He might be out of practice when it came to dating, but he and Carolina got along well, and there was no mistaking the chemistry between them. The longer they were together, the harder it was to keep his hands to himself.

Night after night, date after date, whether they went out or stayed in, even if he only saw her for a few minutes on her work breaks, every second they spent together deepened their connection.

He'd met her parents and the other sisters, and now Sunday mornings were spent side by side at church surrounded by her family and Jake's, with everyone watching them. Carolina might be a mix of tornado and hurricane, but he liked her work ethic, energy, and the effort she put into all of the jobs she held. Most of all, he liked her interactions with Lucy because they were always patient and encouraging. Lucy's intellect and personality could be daunting at times, but Carolina handled Lucy's idiosyncrasies well.

Silas pulled into Holland's driveway and parked beside Pearl. Holland traveled once again for her job, so he didn't worry about blocking her Audi with his truck.

It had been a long day after a long week on a particularly stressful build, and he looked forward to seeing his girls. Carolina had the day off and she'd volunteered to pick Lucy up after school so that Mak could go to the first football game of the season. It was the first date that would include Lucy, but given the time that had gone by and the lack of issues between Carolina and himself, Silas felt it was time to include his daughter. Luce would also serve as a chaperone.

Silas made his way up the stairs, deciding he wasn't going to wait any longer. He was going to tell Carolina how important she was to him—them—tell her he loved her and wanted more.

No one answered his knock on the glass door. He tested the handle, frowning when it opened with a twist. He let himself into the house and listened but heard no signs of Carolina or Lucy. "Hello? Anybody home?"

It was a beautiful day. Not as hot as it had been. Maybe they'd gone up to the crow's nest. He hadn't thought to look when he'd pulled into the drive to see if they were outside.

He heard a sound from upstairs and stilled. But when it came again and he recognized Lucy's voice, he took the stairs two at a time to the bedrooms upstairs.

He hadn't been inside of Carolina's room since the initial walk-thru before the remodel had taken place, and he shook his head and smiled when he spotted the disorderly chaos inside. Definitely a bit of a hurricane. "Hello? Luce?"

"We're in the closet," Carolina called.

Silas made his way to them as the partially opened door swung wide, and he spotted Lucy wearing one of Carolina's many hats, a black flowy top or dress, a string of pearls that hung to the floor despite being tied up, and break-neck heels. "Wow. Look at you," he said before realizing Lucy quietly cried.

Silas blinked at his daughter's teary face and glanced at Carolina. "Hey… what's going on?"

"I don't want her to go!"

Silence followed his daughter's statement, mostly because he wasn't sure what to say. His gaze shifted from his daughter to Carolina. "What's this about?"

"Carolina's leaving! She's going away and we'll never see her again!" Lucy released his legs and stepped out of the shoes as she moved to the closet wall, where she grabbed the map and yanked. The map ripped and pins flew and Lucy let out a wail that tore his heart in two.

"I hate you!"

"Hey! Lucy, come here," he ordered. Silas grabbed hold of Lucy before she could do any more damage or hurt herself with all of the pins. Lucy buried her head against his shoulder and sobbed.

Carolina got to her feet, her cell phone clutched in her hands. She shoved it into the back pocket of her cutoff shorts.

"I'm sorry. Silas… Lucy, please, don't cry. Let me explain."

Silas plucked Lucy up as he straightened, ignoring the hat that dropped to the floor as he cradled his daughter against his chest. "Baby-girl, stop crying. Listen, just because Carolina is going away for a few weeks doesn't mean we won't see her again."

"But we *can't* see her." Lucy sobbed so hard her little body quaked against him.

Silas barely managed to bite back a groan. He'd had a long day, and between the meltdown and the expression Carolina now wore, he had a feeling the evening was about to get longer. "What's she talking about?"

Carolina inhaled and wet her lips. "I… got a new job."

"I didn't think you were looking after you picked up hours at the gift shop on top of everything else."

"It's… I applied before. Months ago. Getting hired is such a long shot, and I didn't mention it because I didn't know if it would ever happen, but they called today and—"

"She's moving to Thailand!"

The air left his lungs in a rush and his blood froze in his veins. "*What?*"

"I'm so sorry," Carolina whispered.

"She won't be here for my presentation with Samuel at school or my birthday or my piano recital or anything!"

He stared at Carolina, glad he had Lucy to hold on to because he read Carolina's expression and knew his daughter's words were true. Carolina was leaving. He squeezed his daughter tighter, wishing his little girl was strong enough to hold him together. "You don't think applying for jobs *overseas* was something you should've told me?"

"It was such a long shot. I should've said something, but why bother when I didn't think—"

"No, you were thinking—of yourself."

"Silas, *please.*"

He'd turned and carried Lucy into the bedroom. Now he stood staring at the chaos he'd considered a part of Carolina's beautiful mess that was only… a mess. "What was I to you? Something to help you pass the time?"

"No. Of course not."

Shock rolled through him, sucking him down like a riptide. Silas stopped short of the threshold, wishing today hadn't been the day of discovery when it came to Carolina's plans. Or his love for her. "I knew you planned to go on a trip. I figured you'd be gone a few weeks, maybe a month. I thought… I thought since things between us had… I didn't think you'd want to be away from us for too long." A rough laugh left him. What a fool he'd been. Again.

"Silas, I never intended to deceive you. To hurt you."

"What did you think this would do to me? To us?"

"Silas, please. I've spent the last *two years* applying for these jobs. It's my *dream*. Do you just expect me to turn it down?"

He paused, her word slicing through him like a knife. "No. I don't. Go. Lucy and I are the last thing that'll hold you back, but then... we wouldn't have held you back either way, now, would we? You've already made your decision."

"I don't want it to be this way," she said softly.

"It wouldn't have been, Carolina, had you told us before my daughter and I fell in love with you."

Chapter 19

Dream catcher. NOW.

The moment the text went out that night alerting the sisters to trouble, Carolina knew there was no turning back.

Holland had returned home from her work trip to find Carolina standing in the middle of the living room staring at the computer screen of images flashing on the kitchen desk. Not crying. Not talking. Just standing. Hurricane Caro had stalled, and according to Holland, it was terrifying.

Holland dropped her bags, pulled out her phone, and thirty minutes later, Holland and Carolina sat on the sand beside the dream catcher mailbox, waiting on the rest of the sisters to arrive.

Frankie got there first.

"Hey, I was elbow deep in an engine. What's going on?" Frankie asked as she dropped to the sand beside Carolina.

Carolina didn't take her gaze off of the surf, because she had a pretty good idea of how the next hour or so of conversation was going to go. They'd take Silas's side. All of them would. And she'd be left defending her dreams like always. Which made her mad and sad. On top of the sad she already felt because she was pretty sure her heart had shattered into a billion pieces when Silas carried his sobbing baby girl out the door.

"Wait," Holland said simply.

London arrived last, wearing a T-shirt that read *Coffee: the anti-murder juicy juice.*

"Hey, you're back," London said to Holland. "How was Tokyo?"

"Noisy."

"Anyone gonna tell us what's going on?" Frankie divided her attention between Carolina and Holland. "Caro's silence is freaking me out. That's just not normal."

London nudged her twin and gave her a small shake of her head.

"Well, it's not."

"I actually don't know what happened," Holland admitted, ending the bickering, "but Carolina is going to tell us. Right, kiddo?"

That shifted four sets of eyes in her direction, and Carolina dug her hands deeper into the sand beneath her.

"Seriously, why isn't she talking? Who broke her?" Frankie said, hands fisted like she was ready to go to battle on Carolina's behalf. And she would. Frankie was the toughest of them all, the defender of anyone weak or defenseless, be it human or animal.

"Has something happened with Silas?" This question came from London. "That's it, isn't it? You two have been spending a lot of time together, and I never did buy that excuse that it was just because you've been babysitting his daughter."

"None of us did," Ireland said. "Caro?"

She inhaled and said a quick prayer that somehow she could make sense of the timing of things. Did Silas still believe everything happened for a reason? If that was true, how did this fit in except to cause horrific pain? "We had a fight. A big one."

"Ahh, the first fight of a relationship. Those are always huge," London stated with a knowing nod of her head.

"There is no relationship. After tonight I'll never see him again." Tears stung her eyes just making the statement, and she blamed the wind coming off the surf. But once they formed, she couldn't blink them away fast enough, and she ducked her head into her knees.

"Hey, whatever it is, you can work through it," Ireland said. "Tell us what happened."

Frankie stretched out a hand and grasped Caroline's ankle. "Yeah. Tell us so we know why we're beating him up."

Carolina forced her head up but found her gaze locked with Holland's. "I told him I got news today."

"About?" Frankie asked.

Carolina curled her arms tighter around her raised knees. "I got the job. One of the ones I've been applying for. I'm a professional house sitter as of tonight. I fly to Thailand next week.

Frankie muttered something the wind carried away.

Carolina breathed in the salt air and stared at her sisters, meeting their gazes one by one. "Don't everyone jump for joy at once."

"We're happy for you," Holland said.

"No, you're not. You don't want me to go." She shoved her hair back from her face, using the motion to discreetly wipe the moisture from her eyes, and groaned. "*How* is it possible to be *so* happy and *so* angry at the same time?"

"What did Silas say?" Holland asked.

"He said I should've told him and Lucy before they fell in love with me."

"Oh, wow."

"Poor guy."

"Poor little girl," Ireland said.

Lucy… Carolina closed her eyes and still heard Lucy's sobs. "I should've handled it better but I answered the call and Lucy was there. She could hear them. It was awful. I was trying to talk to her—to explain—when Silas came and picked her up." She'd never forget his expression. The hurt and betrayal that had so deeply etched his features.

"Love changes things," London added. "Maybe you can work this out?"

"Or change your plans," Ireland stated bluntly. "Some things are more important, Carolina."

"*Why* are you all so against me doing this? Why can't you support me? Do you know how long I've waited for an opportunity like this? How long I've prayed for this to happen?"

"Hey, we will always love and support you, but we're afraid for you," London said.

"You're looking at it like this big adventure, and it is. In a perfect world, the idea of house-sitting as a way to travel is great," Frankie added. "But there are seriously dangerous people in this world who'll take one look at you and see an opportunity to cash in."

"That's true," Holland murmured. "I understand the desire to travel. I love my job and where it sends me, but I'd be lying if I said I didn't get nervous sometimes because of the way some people look at me. It isn't right to be judged as an object to be used, but women face this reality every single day—*especially* overseas. American women have no clue how protected we've been, but all of the sex trafficking stuff happening here now has been happening around the world for centuries."

"Kidnapping and ransoms are always a thing, too," Frankie added. "And Americans traveling alone make for easy targets. Just because it's a nice house somewhere doesn't mean you'd be safe, and we're too far away to do anything if you need us."

"I think the real question is whether or not you love Silas."

The softly spoken comment came from Ireland. "I..." *so totally love him.* But was she willing to give up her dream for him? She worked so hard to be able to do what she wanted. Spent the last two *years* applying for the chance. Was she really going to give up her dream job because of—

"It's a simple question, Caro," London pressed. "Do you or not?"

She inhaled again. Squeezed her arms tighter. "*Why do I have to choose?* That's not fair. Seriously... why?" Yeah, she knew she sounded like a whiny child but it's how she felt. It wasn't fair. Why couldn't she have both? "How could this happen now? And why can't Silas understand how much this means to me?"

"Mama always says God's got a funny sense of humor."

"Yeah, well, this isn't funny. It's everything I've ever wanted, but suddenly I'm the bad guy? And what about that? If I was a man, would you guys support me then?"

"You're fighting something you can't change, Caro. You're *not* a man. Period. And, yes, we'd still be concerned because we love you. But Silas is a working single dad with a school-age child who depends on him for stability, provision, and love," Ireland said firmly. "He is her everything and her needs have to come first because that's what parents *do*."

"I know that."

"Do you?" London asked. "Hey, Cooper's kids are mine now, and they depend on me as much as he does, so I'm just going to say it. You and Silas have dated all summer, and you've filled in the gaps for him with his little girl. You've eaten meals together, worked on *homework* together," she said, referencing the summer school project the kids had worked so hard on. "You've played a huge role in their lives for months, and now you're saying you want him—*them*—to what? Wait for you while you go do your thing and come back when you want? And then what? Pick up where you left off before you leave again? How is that fair to *them*? The man said he loves you but do you love him?"

"Yes, okay? I love him, but——"

"But?"

Everyone waited. And waited. But she didn't have an answer. She glared at her older sister, knowing exactly what that "something" was after the time she'd spent with Silas and his beautiful little girl. "Just because y'all are against it doesn't make it a bad idea. What if I wanted to join the military? Frankie did and everyone was so proud of her."

"Frankie is different."

"Why? Hmm?" She knew she shouldn't press it but she couldn't let the matter drop. Maybe she was upset and angry. But Silas had messed with her brain and her heart and brought all kinds of thoughts to the surface. "Why does she get a pass?"

"For one, what you're talking about doing is different than joining the military. You won't have an entire base at your six if you get into trouble," she said, sounding like a true military brat, "and another, Caro, you're *you*."

Ah, the truth comes out. "Which means you don't think I can do it."

"I never said that."

"But it's what you think. It's what *all* of you think just because I'm a little ADHD."

"A little?"

Ireland elbowed Frankie and glared.

"All I'm saying is that they make medication that will help you focus."

"Medication that has *horrible* side effects. Not only does it——"

"Help you focus," London repeated.

"Make me *unable* to focus on anything else. It's like I have tunnel vision and I have no creativity!"

"You don't have to have a million browsers open and going at the same time, kid. Slow is better than having to redo things because—"

"I'm a screw-up?"

"Oh, you *are* spoiling for a fight, aren't you?" London pointed her finger at Carolina. "Stop it. You're not a screw-up and you know it. Living in a slower gear—otherwise known as being on 'island time'—isn't a bad thing. That's all. Got it?"

Carolina shoved her hands into her hair and pushed it out of her face, knowing in her heart of hearts it was true and London was right.

Ever since she'd opened her eyes this morning, something had seemed off, and all of that energy and "offness" tore through her like a tsunami. She should've let the call go to voicemail. If she had, Lucy wouldn't have overheard the conversation, and maybe things wouldn't have blown up with Silas. Maybe they could've talked. *Like you could have from the beginning had you told him?* "I *like* being busy and creative, and even you can't argue that I'm calm in crazy situations *because* my brain fires so fast and I can get the job done when no one else can."

"Yes, you're right. But what about the other days when you forget to do what you're supposed to do because you're so distracted by any little thing?"

"What about it?"

"Carolina, what if you get over there and you lose focus? Something bad could happen. Really bad. You could do major damage, and the people who own those outrageously expensive houses aren't going to shrug it off as cute and creative."

"Houses have insurance." Wow. Really? That was her defense?

"Fine. Forget the houses. What about when you're exploring on your own? Your fast-firing brain could put you in danger because you go from A to Z without even considering what's happening at all the stops in between."

"That could happen anywhere."

"You're right. It could. But here, we can help you. Caro, we just… worry about you."

"Because everyone still treats me like the baby of the family even though I'm an adult."

"No, because we love you," Holland said. "And like it or not, the ADHD thing is nothing to sneeze at."

"Gee, it must be nice to be perfect."

"Girlie, I am so far from perfect. But all of us can tell some days are worse than others with you—like today. Am I right?"

Lah, she hated it when London was right. "I can't help it."

"We *know*. We get it, but you can't let your ADHD put you at risk."

Carolina rolled her eyes but deep down it angered her. Why couldn't she have been more like her sisters? They all had their acts together and prescription drugs weren't required. All four of them owned or managed businesses, were respected by their peers, whereas she… *did everything they'd mentioned.* Today had been a bad day from start to finish, starting with forgetting to turn the shower off this morning only to be alerted by Lucy when they'd gone upstairs to play after school.

In the past, she'd found her purse in the refrigerator when she'd gone looking for the coffee creamer. And yesterday morning, she'd forgotten to blow out a candle and it had burned all day in Holland's house, where she'd lived rent-free since the hurricane. What if it had caught fire? Hurt one of them?

"Caro, you're supercharged and you like it. But what happens when you wake up one day and realize you've never slowed down enough to appreciate the calm and beauty that's around you?"

"I enjoy calm and beauty. That's part of my reasons for wanting to be a house sitter. I want to travel and have experiences I can't afford otherwise. I don't make enough money to go and stay the way I want to, and this way would let me."

"But why does it have to mean taking on a job overseas away from everything you know and everyone who loves you?"

"Maybe because I get tired of hearing about all of the fun places we went before Dad retired and moved Stateside, and I don't remember them. I was too little but all of you have these great memories from adventures I wasn't a part of because of my age. What's wrong with me wanting to see those places as an adult so that I actually know what you're talking about?"

"If that's truly what this is about, how about we take some girl trips?"

Girl trips. Fun, but not what she had in mind. Ireland and Holland would schedule every moment down to the second, and Frankie and London would worry about being away from their businesses. Not to mention… "I'm pretty sure Dominic and Cooper wouldn't be happy their *wife* and girlfriend are taking off on them so soon. Besides, I'm not talking about a week or two weeks at some resort. I'm talking about staying long enough to really get into the culture. *What?*" Carolina glared at her sisters.

"What are you searching for, Caro? Or running from?" London asked. "Because there's obviously something."

She blinked at the question. "I-I… I don't know, I just

feel like I'm missing something. Something you guys all have." She groaned, uncomfortable with the fact she'd just admitted that aloud. "Why couldn't I have been older? Born first?"

London met Carolina's gaze.

"Oh, hon. You are way too young for a midlife crisis."

"That's too bad because I'm pretty sure I'm having one."

"Caro…" Ireland brushed her hand over Carolina's hair. "What if the question isn't whether or not you love Silas but whether or not you love him *enough* to put his and his daughter's needs before your own? Because that's what this boils down to. That's love and marriage and—"

"He hasn't asked me to marry him. I'm just… We're just… I don't know what we are—were." But they'd been more than friends, that much was certain.

"Yeah, you do. You just don't want to admit it because it means making a choice and possibly reevaluating things," London said.

"It's not fair. The assignment is for five months. There's even a stipend to go along with housing because I guess it's cool to have an American house-sitting there. The stipend covers what I'd be losing cash-wise."

"Well, good for you but what about the rest of us?" Ireland asked. "You're not only walking out on us as a family but also the jobs provided to you. Jobs we count on you to perform."

She groaned aloud. Leave it to Ireland to throw down the responsibility card on top of everything else. "Do you *know* how long I've waited for this opportunity?"

"You wanted Australia, Europe, Scotland, and Italy, if memory serves," London countered. "Not Thailand."

"It gets my foot in the door."

"And slams the rest on them," Frankie said, nodding toward London and Ireland. "Have you planned ahead?

When you get back, who's going to hire you knowing you've left your own family in the lurch?"

"I..." *hadn't considered that.* Silas was right. She *had* only thought of herself.

"Caro, traveling is an option for you. Not a requirement. Only you can choose because, of all the people in this scenario, you're the only one with options. But if you choose to do this, own the consequences without complaint. And for pity's sake, let Silas find someone willing to do what you can't. Don't make it harder on them," Ireland said. "I know what it's like to be considered an *option*, and it's not something I'd wish on anyone."

Well, there it was. She knew where they stood. Knew Ireland's words were right on the mark. The day Silas had told her about his ex's betrayal, she'd been angry on their behalf, but now that anger was mired in her own desires.

After all, how hard could it be to choose between one half of her heart and the other?

Chapter 20

The following afternoon, Silas slammed the truck door with enough force to rattle the windows. The hourly hire behind the wheel looked at him with surprise, and Silas shook his head and waved the kid to get going back to the worksite.

He turned and found the owner of Frankie's Garage watching him with a level stare. "Wind caught it."

"Mmm. The invoice is in my office. Jake sent payment?"

Silas pulled the check from his pocket. "Got it right here."

He followed Carolina's sister into the building and found himself more than a little surprised by the orderliness until he remembered Frankie's military background. The walls held several posters supporting veterans, and PTSD informational brochures were displayed in a clear plastic container at the checkout.

"Gimme a sec. My receptionist is on her lunch break and we updated the system."

Silas handed her the check and waited while Frankie

slowly clicked through the computer screens to print out a receipt. "Thanks," he said when she handed it over.

"She's worth it, you know. The wait, I mean. Maybe if you thought of it like a deployment..."

Silas stared down at the paper for a long moment before shifting his gaze back to the dark-haired woman. The family resemblance was remarkable except for Frankie's coloring, so opposite of her light-haired, light-complected twin, London. "It's dangerous."

"Lots of things are these days. Look, I don't like it either. None of us do. She's... scattered and unobservant on a good day. But it's important to her. She believes travel will help her grow as a person."

"Then she should go."

"And maybe you could call her."

"If she wants to talk, she knows where I am."

"Ah, Mr. Tough Guy. Careful with that ego. You might trip on it."

Taken aback by the woman's forthrightness, Silas frowned. "Ego has nothing to do with it."

"No? If not ego, then what?"

Frankie's gaze narrowed on him with such intensity he wanted to step back, get in the fixed truck, and leave. "History," he heard himself say.

Dawning understanding crossed the woman's features, and he hated that he'd revealed more than he'd wanted with a single word.

"Your baby mama?"

He nodded and lifted his free hand to his face, rubbing his fingers over his chin. "I learned a long time ago that you can't make someone love you. Or stay if they don't want to."

"But you love Carolina?"

He thought about that. Tried to pinpoint the moment when his interest and curiosity and desire for her had formed into something more. "Yeah, I do. She… changed things. Made me realize there's a piece of the puzzle missing."

"And she's the piece?"

"Yeah."

"Might want to remember that."

"I'm not following."

"If she's the piece that's missing, it's going to be hard to find another piece to fit then, isn't it? So you might want to stick with the piece you know fits."

Silas held out his hand. "She knows how to contact me. Keys?"

A WEEK LATER, Carolina placed the last of her luggage in the pile and took a step back, digging her phone out of her pocket to go over her list again. She had set reminders for everything, like when to take her medication—because, after conceding there might be a need for it and seeing the difference it made, she figured she would be better off not killing her employer's plants, forgetting to feed their dog, or burning down their house if she left a candle burning. Any one of those things could result in her not getting a good recommendation, and her first house-sitting job might be her last.

She'd surprised herself this week by getting ready for her international adventure with no help from her family. They offered because they always offered, but she'd turned them down knowing the planning and preparation was something she needed to do on her own.

Her phone chimed and a drop screen appeared—the reminder of Lucy and Samuel's special project presentation at school. Her heart skipped a beat at the news, and she bit her lower lip hard to stem the instant flood of tears.

"The car will be here any second."

Carolina turned and found Holland descending the stairs carrying her sleek designer suitcase and matching carry-on. Holland was dressed for the meeting she headed to in upstate New York and looked chic and sophisticated, whereas Carolina had gone boho and maybe a little too *un*sophisticated?

No. She was who she was. Maybe it was the medication or her belief in herself or a combination of the two, but her confidence had changed over the last week, despite her heartbreak and all the tears she'd shed for a man who'd kept his distance even though she'd seen him at school during pickup times.

Since they were both heading to the airport, Holland had gotten a car for them so no one else in the family would have to miss the event at school. Her dad had stopped by this morning to say goodbye while her mom had cried her way through the going-away dinner held for her last night. Ireland had hugged her last night before leaving to sneak over to the house she and Dominic had bought as a wedding present, still pretending she and Dominic were only engaged rather than already married so their mother could have the wedding she wanted. Frankie had hugged her, too, and made her promise to watch her six and never let her guard down, even for a second. Silas and Lucy had been invited but hadn't attended the dinner.

"You're thinking awfully hard over there. Everything okay?"

"You've *never* had your toes curled?"

Holland tilted her head to one side and smiled. "Nope."

"Am I making a mistake?"

"I dunno. Are you?"

Carolina inhaled and turned her head to stare at her

sister. "Why did you buy a house here? Why not in New York or Paris or somewhere your company has a home office?"

Holland put her ever-present cell phone away in a pocket and waved Carolina over to the swing placed in the shade beneath the house. They sat down and Holland put the swing in motion, but all Carolina could do was think how odd it was to see Holland dressed in her professional suit and heels sitting on the old-fashioned swing.

"Because even though I travel a lot, I don't want to miss out on even more. Home is where your heart is, and my heart, at least for now, is here with you and the fam."

"So if you meet someone, you'll move away?"

Holland laughed softly and shrugged. "Caro, I have no idea. You know as well as I do that's not up to me."

"But you'd have to make a choice."

"I would. But I'll cross that bridge when it appears."

Carolina leaned her head back and released a deep groan. "I give up."

"You give up, what?"

"Everything. All of it. I give! Why does it have to be so hard when I finally have what I've always wanted?"

"Is it what you want?"

She opened her mouth to say yes but the word wouldn't form. She inhaled and tried again but— "Why can't I have both? I love him, Hol. I really, really do. This *sucks*. I just wish I'd get a sign and I'd stop being so torn and I'd know what to—"

Her phone chimed again and Carolina flipped it over to see the drop-down alert appear. *Lucy's Presentation. Don't miss it!*

Holland read the alert before it disappeared and laughed.

"A sign, huh?"

She closed her eyes and groaned again. "That was me. Not some higher power."

"Timing is everything, kiddo."

"But… Thailand."

"Caro, get on the plane. Don't get on the plane. That's up to you. But the fact you're so torn about this means something. Don't you think?"

A black town car pulled into the driveway and rolled to a stop. The well-dressed driver got out and Holland said hello and stood.

"Time's up. Make or break."

She followed Holland to the car and watched as the driver loaded her luggage before climbing into the backseat behind her sister.

"You two all set in there?" the driver asked, hunching down to see them.

"Yes."

Carolina inhaled. "Yes."

The driver shut the door, and in seconds, they backed out and were on their way to the airport.

"Looks like there's been an accident up ahead. I'll have to go another way."

"That's fine. We have a time buffer," Holland said, looking down at her phone.

Carolina stared out the window at the passing scenery, and with every block, the vise on her chest tightened. She pulled off her hat and used it to fan her hot face, then tossed it aside and grabbed her phone to check her list one more time. Passport, cash, debit card, ID, address for the house—

A chime sounded and an alert box appeared. *Lucy's presentation*. It was time for it to begin. "Go faster."

"Pardon?" the driver asked.

"Caro? You okay?"

"No. Go faster. T-take a right. Go around the lake. To the school. Go!"

"Yes, ma'am."

The driver gunned the engine and the car shot forward. He slowed at the stop signs but didn't stop, and she forced herself not to yell at the man because he wasn't doing sixty in a twenty-five. *Go, go, go!*

She couldn't look at Holland. Didn't know what she was doing, planning to do once she got there. She just knew she had to—

"It's blocked. They're doing construction. I can only turn left."

Carolina sucked in a sharp breath and opened the door.

"Miss!"

"Caro, the car's moving—"

The driver slammed on the brakes.

She jumped out of the car and ran, toward the school a block away. She had one more street to cross. The school was up ahead, kids, parents, and staff mingling at the door. She wasn't too—

Brakes squealed, the sound jerking her out of the panicked haze.

"Lady, I almost hit— *Carolina?*"

Carolina gulped when she felt the heat of the large truck because it was so close. She'd been so focused on getting to the school she'd run right out into the road without looking.

"Carolina?"

Silas's angry voice jarred her, but his hands settling on her arms and shoulders brought her the rest of the way to awareness.

"Are you *trying* to get yourself killed?"

She stared up at him, teary-eyed and laughing and shaking her head at her crazy self. "I love you."

He blinked.

"What?"

"I love you," she said again. "I-I should've told you sooner but I didn't and then you got so angry and left. But… I love you. You and Lucy."

Silas looked as though he wanted to strangle her and smile at the same time, and she hated that she was the reason he was so torn.

"Aren't you supposed to be getting on a plane? What about Thailand?"

Yeah, what about Thailand? Was she really going to give it up? She swallowed hard, fear and hope and sheer determination filling her eyes with tears at the thought of him rejecting her and walking away again. "Holland said she's never moved away because her heart is here and I realized… mine is, too. You and Lucy and my family. I want to travel but I can't just up and leave. You. Them. My jobs. I-if I can get the company to give me another assignment later in the year, would you go with me? Not now. But when you and Lucy are able. H-holidays or winter months— Whenever we could go *together*. Would you consider it?"

Silas's hands tightened on her arms, and he tugged her closer, up onto her tiptoes, all the while lowering his head slowly until their breaths mingled and she could see the wariness and the hope in his eyes.

"The things you'll do to get my attention," he murmured, his eyes narrowed. "Stealing my parking space, jumping out in front of my truck—"

"Falling in love with you," she added, breathless.

"That, too."

He brushed his lips over hers, and the moment her lips parted, he lifted her off her feet and deepened the kiss. Cars honked and she vaguely heard catcalls and whistles from the adults at the school, but she didn't care. She held on to her heart and kissed him with all of the love bursting inside of her. Compromise was a thing. And sometimes it was everything.

"I love you, sweetheart."

Carolina hugged Silas tight and focused on the moment. The scent of him, the sight of him. The love she felt in his strength. Her new map of dreams would have a new pin, a special pin.

One that marked home with all of the love that held her here.

THE SEASIDE SISTERS SERIES CONTINUES WITH WORTH THE RISK. KEEP READING FOR A SHORT EXCERPT:

"FRANKIE?"

She shook her dark head, an incredulous huff leaving her chest as she shoved a box toward him. He dropped his wallet in his effort to secure the box and stared, pulse racing in his veins as she turned without a word and headed toward the stairs. "Frankie, wait. Frankie!"

He tossed the box onto the closest outdoor chair and chased after her, grasping her arm gently to stop her.

A dog began barking and jumped out of an old Jeep, racing toward them.

"You wanna keep that hand, you'd better let go."

He released her immediately and stepped back from the growling dog at her side. "Just… wait a second, okay? Who's your friend?"

"Tank. And why should I wait? The wifey-poo not home to see you flirting with me, so you feel safe?"

He bit back a curse and fought to control his temper. She wouldn't listen a year and a half ago either, but this time… "No, she's—"

"You're *unbelievable*."

The dog's growls got louder, but it didn't move from its spot at her side, even when she lowered her hand to its head.

"She's *dead*, Frankie." Maybe it was a cheap shot by way of insensitivity, but he had to say something to slow her down before she disappeared like she had last time.

He held her gaze, flummoxed like he always was every time he came into contact with her. She was thinner than he remembered but just as beautiful as ever. Her dark brown hair was pulled back from her face in a pony, and unlike earlier today when he'd seen her—if it had been her—she now wore standard-issue olive green shorts and a camo T-shirt.

"Should I give my condolences or congratulate you? I'm a little confused."

And angry. He tilted his head toward the door. "Want to come in?"

"No."

"Will you come in?" he asked next. "I'd like to talk to you and I'd rather not have this discussion in front of my neighbors."

"What are you *doing* here, Grayson?"

A smile pulled at the corners of his lips despite the seriousness of her expression. He shook his head and glanced at the box she'd brought with her. Wait, was that his— "I could ask you the same thing. Where did you get that?"

"Apparently a kid brought it to my garage today to sell. Said his dad was a sick vet with cancer and needed the money."

Christopher. Grayson fisted his hands and his anger must have radiated off of him, because Tank released another warning growl.

"Your dog has issues."

"He's a retired WMD and he doesn't like it when people yell at me."

"I didn't yell at you."

"I guess he just doesn't like you then."

"What did the kid look like?" It was a stupid question since he was pretty sure those types of parts weren't just lying around in garages at the beach, but asking the question bought him some time.

"I didn't see him. One of my mechanics made the deal. Got it for less than half price, so I figured something was fishy. He'd overlooked a packing slip inside. So is it true?"

He blinked at her, not following.

"Do you have cancer?"

Would she care if he did? "No. What I have is apparently a kid who can't seem to stay out of trouble."

Frankie's expression didn't reveal much, but he knew her well enough to know she was as blown away by their reunion as he was. "It's a little weird how we keep winding up together, isn't it?"

A low huff left her ample chest.

"We're not together. And you didn't answer my question. What *are* you doing here?"

"I'm out. I'm a full-time dad working at a local doctor's office and clinic as their PA."

He watched her close her eyes and fist her hands. Apparently she'd hoped he was just visiting? "Frankie—"

"You knew I lived here. *I* was honest and told you about my life. About my home, my family. Where I lived. You didn't think we'd run into each other? That it'd be a problem for you to be here?"

He ignored the shot at his character, because it was deserved, and took a step closer. "Wilmington isn't some Podunk town, Frankie. Toss in the population of the beaches… Okay, yeah, I'd be lying if I said it hadn't crossed my mind that I *might* see you at some point, but we also could've lived here all of our lives and never run into each other."

"How long have you been here?"

He inhaled. "Since April." And it had taken everything inside of him not to track her down any way he possibly could. Through buddies still in the military, through the internet. But given their history, starting a new job, and his rocky relationship with Christopher, Gray knew he'd needed time to settle in. Get his life on an even keel before anything else.

An exasperated huff left her again.

"Frankie… come inside. Please. Let's talk. Let me finally explain."

She squared her shoulders, lifted her chin, one-hundred-percent pissed female ready to do battle. Her expression changed and he kicked himself for the millionth time for not being honest with her from the beginning.

"There's nothing you can say to explain away the lies," she said before purposefully moving down the stairs like insurgents were hot on her heels.

He took a step, going to follow her, but Tank went up on all fours and growled again. "You and I are gonna have to come to terms," he said to the dog.

"Not happening," Frankie called over her shoulder as she reached the bottom step. "But I am glad you don't have cancer."

He watched her go, taking in every sway of her hips and every bounce of her pony. The long, tanned length of her legs and the proud tilt of her head. She got into an old Jeep that gave off an impressive roar when she twisted the key.

Now that his master was safe, Tank took off down the stairs and leaped into the Jeep beside her, sitting tall and proud on the passenger seat.

Grayson couldn't help the small smile that pulled at his lips at the image they made, all rough and tough and protective of one another. But he knew both had a softer side. He'd seen Frankie's and wanted to see it again.

She might hate him, but she was glad he didn't have cancer.

It was a start and he'd take it. And now that she'd made contact and he knew how to find her... he had some making up to do.

THE SEASIDE SISTERS SERIES:

THE LAST GOODBYE
LATTES AND LULLABYES
MAP OF DREAMS
WORTH THE RISK
LOST LOVE FOUND

Books Also Set in Carolina Cove

CAROLINA COVE SERIES:

- SEASCAPES AND VEGAS MISTAKES
- SEASHELLS AND WEDDING BELLS
- SEA GLASS AND SECOND CHANCES
- SEA BLUE AND LOVING YOU
- SEA VIEW AND SOMETHING NEW

MAKE ME A MATCH SERIES:

- ROMANCE RESET
- RULES OF ENGAGEMENT
- THE MATCHMAKER'S SECRET
- PERFECTLY MISMATCHED
- BY THE BOOK

THE SEASIDE SISTERS SERIES:

- THE LAST GOODBYE
- LATTES AND LULLABYES
- MAP OF DREAMS

- WORTH THE RISK
- LOST LOVE FOUND

COMING SOON: (LINKS WILL BE UPDATED ASAP)
THE BLACKWELL BROTHERS SERIES:

- BABY BE MINE
- SECOND CHANCE WEDDING
- THE GETAWAY GUY
- OFF-LIMITS LOVE
- FLIRTING WITH FOREVER

Chapter 1

Hey, I can tell you're exhausted from your week in Vegas but what's up with you?" Amelia asked, sliding Izzy a searching glance from the driver's seat. "I thought you'd be bouncing off the walls with excitement."

Isabel Shipley—Izzy to her friends and family—lifted a hand to rub her upper chest and wondered if it was time to break down and take something for the anxiety plaguing her ever since waking up in her hotel room this morning on her last day in Las Vegas.

The rumpled bed had said a lot of things, but it was the running shower and suddenly pounding head that wouldn't allow her to put two and two together and come up with anything other than sheer panic. Especially when a glance at the bedside clock gave her barely an hour to get to the airport and through Vegas security for her flight back home to Carolina Cove, North Carolina.

Given her frantic state to get out while the gettin' was good, she'd scrambled into clothes she'd purposely left out because she *always* ran late and grabbed the suitcase she had haphazardly packed the day before on a break from the gallery. After a last horrified glance at the open bathroom door and the scrumptiousness she left behind, she'd made a run for the hills and hopefully the return of her sanity.

She didn't *do* things like this. Ever.

So why had she?

Adrenaline had given her just enough mindfulness to hail a taxi, but the TSA line was long and she'd had to freaking *run* for her gate, arriving mere seconds before the door to the plane shut behind her as the last one to board.

Head throbbing from the stress ice pick stabbing her brain, she'd curled up against the window, her mind racing with questions and embarrassment as memories of the previous night surfaced until she fell into a fitful doze that came from too much stress, not enough sleep, a physical soreness that brought a blush to her cheeks.

Hours after leaving the hotel room and Vegas behind, her mind still hadn't come up with any logical answers. Truthfully, she couldn't even blame the champagne she'd drunk.

She'd only had three glasses over a span of time, but her excitement and adrenaline had known no bounds. And what better way to celebrate the completion of her first *real* showcase than with a tall, dark, and very gorgeous man?

He'd made her tingle. Like, seriously, *tingle*. She hadn't known such a thing was possible. Even more amazing, he'd seemed genuinely interested in her art and process, which was *such* a turn-on itself.

He also knew her cousin Michael and had attended her showcase because of it—which made him safer than the average Joe.

"Izzy? Seriously, you're worrying me. What's up?" her best friend asked.

Izzy watched as Amelia ran a hand over her rapidly expanding belly in a soothing-mama gesture and swallowed hard. She had to snap out of it. If anyone should be freaking out, it was Amelia. She was the one with twins on the way.

Izzy nodded to herself. *Suck it up, buttercup.* What was done was done. She and Everett had flirted, sipped luscious champagne, played blackjack and…made a bet. Which was how she'd wound up listening to the shower spray in the next room.

Winner gets a kiss, he'd said.

Loser has to— "I-I…I'm fine. Just really, *really* tired." Because while her challenge hadn't been anything outrageous, it *had* led to the aftermath.

"But your show was a success? You texted and said you'd scored some good commissions and would text me later to tell me details."

Thankful for the distraction, Izzy turned her attention to the passing scenery. "Yeah, sorry about that. I went to the bar for a drink and…talked to friends."

Friend, rather. That's where she'd met him again. The handsome not-so-stranger who'd wandered through the gallery around each of her paintings as though looking over a Monet or something equally amazing. Everett had introduced himself as a longtime friend of her cousin Michael's, said that he'd seen her name on the signs about the gallery show, and remembered Michael bragging about his talented artist cousin and the timing of her upcoming show.

They'd chatted briefly, her entire body humming with excitement because he was so…*so fine.*

But it wasn't until later when she'd met up with him in the bar that things had gone from casual conversation to major flirtation.

"I thought as much. You know, sometimes it really comes down to the people you know, which is why it's so important to get out there. So? Tell me. Who bought your work? Anyone famous?"

Izzy frowned. She'd stayed so busy in Las Vegas prepping for the show after the last-minute inclusion that she hadn't had time to miss home. But now that she was here?

The familiar sights and traffic signs pointing to Carolina Cove brought tears to her eyes and comfort to her soul.

Or maybe it was the relief that she could almost shut herself inside her apartment and pretend the last twelve hours hadn't happened?

Or relive them.

To be honest, it was a toss-up as to which she'd prefer.

How could a thirty-two-year-old woman get herself into such a pickle?

God forbid she ever admit this, but maybe her mother was right? She was too old for this. The games that came with dating and…

It's not dating when it's a one-night stand.

Which she didn't do.

Ever.

Except with someone Michael knows?

Her cousin wasn't a saint by any means, but she was pretty sure he wouldn't want to go to a business meeting and find out what had happened to his "kid cousin" in Vegas. And if memory served, Michael and Everett were currently working on a project.

Great. Oh, great.

"Iz?"

She had to really focus to remember Amelia's question. "Um, I-I don't know. The buyers finalized everything with the curator. I'll get more details this week, I'm sure. There...wasn't much time there at the end." Because she'd finished the show floating on a cloud, having made plans to meet Everett to celebrate the completion.

"Well, it's fantastic. I'm so proud of you," Amelia said, sliding Izzy another glance from across the way as she crossed the bridge toward Carolina Cove.

"Thanks. I mean, they could always change their mind but—"

"No buts. It's awesome and doubtful that would happen, so accept the sales as a win. I'm happy for you."

"Yeah. It's just...surreal." *In so many ways.*

She appreciated Amelia's support. Her friend was the best, softhearted and understanding and supportive even though Izzy's crazy ideas weren't always thought through.

"Okay, so, you're only minutes away from home. Take today off to recoup and rest, and then you can hit the ground running tomorrow."

"Yeah, I think I might." Sleep was good. It would bring clarity. Right? Maybe then she could figure out exactly how she'd gone from being a not-so-wild child to waking up with a virtual stranger.

She'd had boyfriends. Two long-term ones and a handful of wannabes. But despite what people—especially her mother—might believe about artists and her so-called bohemian lifestyle, she wasn't a casual hookup kind of girl.

And other than talking and laughing and kissing—a *lot* —she wasn't sure when the scales had tipped during the night. Only that she'd allowed Everett to walk her to her hotel room in the wee hours of the morning after all their fun—and then invited him inside.

"Thanks again for picking me up."

"Absolutely. The timing couldn't have worked out better. I can drop you off and head to the film location to look around and still make it home early. I want to do something special for Lincoln's birthday. Especially since this is our last birthday alone for a while."

Izzy watched as Amelia slid her hand over her pregnant belly again and loved how happy her friend seemed to be. Pregnancy definitely agreed with her. "Good thing I have my sunglasses on," she teased. "You're absolutely glowing."

Amelia laughed, her earrings brushing her shoulders as she shrugged.

"I feel like it. I mean, it's weird but I have all of this *energy*. I'm told it's not the norm and usually the opposite is true, but I think I could climb mountains with energy to spare."

Izzy thought of how tired her older sister, Allie, had been during her pregnancies and shook her head. Definitely not the norm. "Just don't overdo it," Izzy said, wishing she could borrow some of that energy right now. Maybe then she wouldn't feel as though she'd been dragged out to sea by a riptide and been swimming against the current for days.

"Oh, I won't. I couldn't if I wanted to. Lincoln has been waiting on me hand and foot when I get home from work, and no one on set will let me lift a finger. Oh! Crap."

"What?"

"Well, before I forget...I ran into the Babes while you were gone."

"And?"

"I hate to say it, but your mom *insists* we use her house for the baby shower you're hosting. I hope that's okay? When I told them we were going to have it downstairs at London's Lattes, the Babes...well, they made it *really* hard to say no."

No doubt they had. The Babes rarely took no for an answer to anything. But why should they when the five older women had been catered to their whole lives?

During the summers of '58 and '59, four prominent Carolina Cove neighbors and friends had given birth to baby girls. One even had a set of twins. The proud mothers had taken the babes for daily strolls in their prams

—and the locals had nicknamed them the Boardwalk Babes—a name used to this day by the now sixty-somethings.

All in all, Izzy had four pseudo aunts and ten "cousins," seven female and three male—with the twin Babes each having a set of twins of their own—ranging in age from mid-forties all the way down to Izzy's thirty-two. Growing up, it had sucked to always be the youngest. Even more so because not only had her two older sisters treated her like the baby but all of her "cousins" had as well. She'd always been the kid sister no one wanted tagging along to dampen their fun.

"Okay," Amelia said, turning down the street toward London's Lattes and pulling to a stop behind Izzy's VW Bug convertible. Betty the Bug might be old, but she was still just as pretty as the day Izzy had bought her. Minus a little sun damage the south was known for.

"Need help getting in?" Amelia asked.

"No. I've got it. Thanks."

Izzy had rented the apartment above the coffee shop a little over a year ago when London Cohen, owner of London's Lattes, had met and then married a northern transplant who'd moved to the beach with his adopted children. Making rent wasn't always easy with her sporadic sales, but there was no denying being on her own gave Izzy a sense of freedom and independence she'd longed for after far too many years under her parents' roof.

Living a minimalist lifestyle made it easier to live sale to sale, but it didn't leave much in the bank afterwards. Not that her parents needed to know that. But thankfully with her commissions from the Vegas showcase, she now had a cushion that would allow her to breathe for at least six months. She would put that time to good use.

Her mother had never understood why Izzy felt the need to move out of their garage apartment into an apartment several blocks away, but Izzy knew if she ever had a hope of proving her abilities and worth, she had to stand on her own. Even if it meant giving up more than a few luxuries. Life was about more than just things. It was experiences and moments…moments she captured and painted because she couldn't imagine doing anything else with her life—no matter what her family said.

"Okay, so get in there and get some rest. You don't seem like yourself, and you'll need all the energy you can muster now that the Babes are involved in the baby shower. I have a feeling things might be a little over-the-top now."

"Ain't that the truth," Izzy muttered, pulling her lips into a wry twist of dread. If her mother and the rest of the Babes knew one thing, it was how to entertain. Nothing could be simple. A party—especially a baby shower welcoming a new life into the world—would be "Babe-ified" in the extreme.

"Sorry. I know I should've protested more, but you know how they can be."

"Trust me, I know," Izzy said truthfully. "And it's not a problem. I'm used to dealing with my mother and the Babes. No worries." While navigating the Babes might make shower prepping more stressful, Izzy wouldn't be responsible for footing the bill on the Babes' many additions to the planning. If nothing else, that was a win for her in a time when she needed to bank and save as much as she could for a rainy day.

"Iz?"

Izzy was halfway out the door when Amelia stopped her. "Yeah?"

"What's with the ring? You're pretty eclectic but that's not exactly your usual style," Amelia said with a wry expression and a little laugh.

Izzy glanced down at the gaudy, sparkling double dice ring she wore on the ring finger of her left hand. One she'd thought about taking off on the plane but hadn't because of the memories it now held in the somewhat sensual-coated space in her brain from last night.

The fun of three glasses of bubbly seemed like a good idea while she had such a great time with a handsome, charismatic man. "Oh, it's just, um, a souvenir," she said, swallowing hard because of the way her heart began to pound in her chest when an image appeared in her mind. The champagne-coated edges of her memories sharpened, and she zeroed in on the moment her gorgeous companion had slid the ring onto her finger, a smile on his seductive lips that she'd matched with one of her own.

"Good thing. For a second there I thought you'd gone and gotten married in Vegas."

Izzy released a laugh that sounded shriller than she'd intended and slid her purse to her shoulder. "You know how it goes. What happens in Vegas stays in Vegas."

SEASCAPES AND VEGAS MISTAKES

Also by Kay Lyons

MONTANA SECRETS SERIES:

- HEALING HER COWBOY
- IT HAD TO BE YOU
- HERS TO KEEP
- MILLION DOLLAR STANDOFF
- HIS CHRISTMAS WISH
- THEIR SECRET SON

THE SEASIDE SISTERS SERIES:

- THE LAST GOODBYE
- LATTES AND LULLABYES
- MAP OF DREAMS
- WORTH THE RISK
- LOST LOVE FOUND

TAMING THE TULANES SERIES:

- SMALL TOWN SCANDAL
- THEIR SECRET BARGAIN
- CROSSING THE LINE
- THE NANNY'S SECRET
- SOMEONE TO TRUST

THE STONE RIVER SERIES:

- WORTH THE WAIT
- NOT BY SIGHT
- THROUGH THE VALLEY
- LEAD ME NOT
- CHRISTMAS AT HOLLY WOOD
- THEIR CHRISTMAS MIRACLE

- SECOND CHANCES

SMALL TOWN SCANDALS SERIES:

- BRODY'S REDEMPTION
- FALLING FOR HER BOSS
- WITH THIS MAN

SECRET SANTA SERIES:

- SECRET SANTA
- SECRET SANTA II: A CHRISTMAS TO REMEMBER

MAKE ME A MATCH SERIES:

- ROMANCE RESET
- RULES OF ENGAGEMENT
- THE MATCHMAKER'S SECRET
- PERFECTLY MISMATCHED
- BY THE BOOK

CAROLINA COVE SERIES:

- SEASCAPES AND VEGAS MISTAKES
- SEASHELLS AND WEDDING BELLS
- SEA GLASS AND SECOND CHANCES
- SEA BLUE AND LOVING YOU
- SEA VIEW AND SOMETHING NEW

COMING SOON: (LINKS WILL BE UPDATED ASAP)

THE BLACKWELL BROTHERS SERIES:

- BABY BE MINE
- SECOND CHANCE WEDDING
- THE GETAWAY GUY
- OFF-LIMITS LOVE
- FLIRTING WITH FOREVER

About the Author

Kay Lyons always wanted to be a writer, ever since the age of seven or eight when she copied the pictures out of a Charlie Brown book and rewrote the story because she didn't like the plot. Through the years her stories have changed but one characteristic stayed true— they were all romances. Each and every one of her manuscripts included a love story.

Published in 2005 with Harlequin Enterprises, Kay's first release was a national bestseller. Kay has also been a HOLT Medallion, Book Buyers Best and RITA Award nominee. Look for her most recent novels with Kindred Spirits Publishing.

For more information regarding her work, please visit Kay at the following:

www.kaylyonsauthor.com

@KayLyonsAuthor (Twitter)

Kay Lyons Author (Facebook)

Author_Kay_Lyons (Instagram)

Kay Lyons, Author (Pinterest)

SIGN UP FOR KAY'S NEWSLETTER AND RECEIVE UPDATES ON NEW RELEASES, CONTESTS, PRE-RELEASE BOOK INFORMATION, EXCLUSIVES AND MORE!